BATTLE OF THE BEACH FREAKS

SAM HAY

Catnip

CATNIP BOOKS
Published by Catnip Publishing Ltd
Quality Court
off Chancery Lane
London WC2A 1HR

First published 2014
1 3 5 7 9 10 8 6 4 2

Text © 2014 Sam Hay
Illustrations © 2014 Tom Morgan-Jones

A CIP catalogue record for this book is available from the British Library

ISBN 978-1-84647-169-8

Printed in Poland

www.catnippublishing.co.uk

Please return/renew this item by the
last date shown to avoid a charge.
Books may also be renewed by phone
and Internet. May not be renewed if
required by another reader.
www.libraries.barnet.gov.uk

LONDON BOROUGH

For Dad

CHAPTER 1

When Gordon Twigg asked my auntie Gloria to marry him, he very nearly killed her. Of course he hadn't meant to. He was just trying to surprise her. But unfortunately his plan went a bit wrong.

It was the end of February, Sunday lunch time at the Golden Wok restaurant. And we were all there – me, my big brother Andy, Mum, Dad, Auntie Gloria and her boyfriend Gordon. He told us later he'd been trying to pluck up the courage to propose for weeks, when suddenly he'd looked across the table, seen something irresistible in the way Auntie Gloria sipped her soup and decided to go for it.

He wanted to make it special. He'd read somewhere about a famous actor who'd surprised his girlfriend with an engagement ring hidden inside her jelly.

Auntie Gloria doesn't like jelly, so Gordon slipped the ring into her chicken noodle soup instead. He thought she'd spot it. But she didn't. Auntie Gloria just spooned up the soup and slurped it down. Or tried to – the ring got stuck in the back of her throat.

For a few ghastly seconds she sat there choking, her face turning purple, then blue, then a scary grey colour. Luckily, my dad was sitting next to her (he's a bus driver and has done loads of first-aid courses because people are always dropping dead on buses). He gave her a hefty thump on the back and the ring shot out like a champagne cork, straight into my lemonade. Plop!

No one knew what to do next. But Auntie Gloria started giggling. And Gordon grinned. And then we all joined in. And suddenly everything was all right again.

After that Gordon did it properly. He fished the ring out of my drink, wiped it on his shirt, got down on one knee and asked Gloria to be his wife. She said, 'Yes!' and then the restaurant went wild. Everyone was shaking Gordon's hand and kissing Auntie Gloria's cheek. And the waiters brought a bottle of champagne, which Dad said they didn't charge us for, and lots of little cakes with syrupy pineapple middles. Then just when I thought the day couldn't get any better, Auntie Gloria turned to me, took my hand and said, 'Of course you'll be my bridesmaid, Jess, won't you . . .'

Wow! It was like a whole box of fireworks had exploded in my belly. I couldn't believe my ears. I'd given up hope of ever being a bridesmaid. Plenty of my mates had done it. But me? No chance. I just didn't have the right relatives. The problem was most of them were happily married, apart from my gran (who's 78 and isn't big on blokes) and my second cousin Connie (who's training to be a mechanic and wouldn't be seen dead in a frilly frock and flowers). No, my only chance of becoming a bridesmaid rested with Auntie Gloria, who had been (unsuccessfully) looking for love for years. But the funny thing was Mr Right has been right under her nose all along . . .

You see Gordon and Gloria actually worked for the same supermarket. She was a bun baker and he served on the fish counter. But they'd never met. Until one evening Gloria had a sudden fancy for fish for tea and their eyes had met over a slice of salmon. They'd been dating ever since. They were actually very well suited. Gordon lived with his mum and wore sensible sweaters and warm socks. Gloria lived with her three cats and knitted sensible sweaters and warm socks. And now they were going to get married.

'You'll help me choose everything, won't you, Jess?' said Auntie Glow, squeezing my hand. 'The flowers, the dresses, the cake . . .'

(Just for the record, we call her Auntie Glow because it's short for Gloria, but mostly because her face lights up like a lantern when she smiles.)

'Of course I'll help,' I grinned. 'I'd love to!'

'Poor Auntie Glow,' muttered Andy from across the table.

I tried to kick him, but he dodged his legs away.

'I'd like to get married on Midsummer's Day,' said Auntie Glow dreamily, 'in a church filled with friends and flowers . . . I'd like a big floaty frock and a horse and carriage . . .'

I shut my eyes and pictured it. So did Mum. We must have looked a bit daft, because when I opened them again, Dad and Andy were making silly faces.

Gordon, meanwhile, was looking slightly sweaty. 'Er, Gloria . . .' he said nervously. 'I was thinking of something smaller . . . a quiet little wedding, just a few friends.'

But Auntie Glow wasn't listening. She'd been waiting for this day for years and wasn't going to settle for anything small. As soon as lunch was finished, she took my arm (and Mum's too) and headed for the nearest newsagents to buy every glossy wedding magazine she could find.

'Oh, look at that dress,' beamed Auntie Glow, flicking through the first one she picked up. 'And that wedding cake.' She pointed to a massive chocolate layer cake, which was bigger than Dad's bus.

Gordon, who had followed us inside the shop,

bobbed nervously in the background, tugging at his tie. 'I don't know, Glow, it all looks a bit fussy . . .'

But Auntie Glow still wasn't listening. 'Oh, look at that bridesmaid's dress. You'd look beautiful in that, Jess.'

It *did* look amazing. Layers and layers of white chiffon and silk, with daisies round the middle.

'Yeah – amazingly like a marshmallow!' smirked Andy, who was peering over my shoulder.

And then Dad, who had tagged along to look at the golf magazines, pointed to the price, 'Four hundred quid for a bridesmaid's dress!'

And Gordon looked like he might faint.

But despite Auntie Glow's plans for a big summer wedding, she soon discovered there was no way she could get married that summer because everything was already booked up, and had been for months.

In fact, the first free weekend Auntie Glow could find was November 1st, the day after Halloween. Andy helpfully suggested Auntie Glow make it a horror-themed wedding. We rolled our eyes, but as I soon discovered, Andy's suggestion wasn't as silly as it sounded . . .

CHAPTER 2

For the next eight months our family was gripped with wedding fever. Dress shopping. Cake tasting. Hymn choosing. Even Dad started humming the wedding march when he was in the shower. And then finally it was Friday afternoon, the day before the wedding. Everything was ready. The church was booked. The cake was baked. And I'd had my outfit hanging in my wardrobe for weeks. Of course I didn't get the dress in the magazine, but mine was just as lovely – rose-coloured satin and silk, ballerina length, with a lavender-coloured sash, glittery shoes and a big silk flower to wear in my hair.

And if there was an award for best-prepared bridesmaid, I reckon I'd have scooped it. You see, since accepting the role, I'd taken it very seriously.

I'd borrowed books from the library, read all Auntie Glow's magazines and I'd put together a scrapbook called 'Everything You'll Ever Need to Know About Being a Bridesmaid'. To be honest, I'd been boring my mates stupid about the wedding for weeks. And as I waved them goodbye at the school gates, I was already planning the PowerPoint 'Show and Tell' I'd be doing at school the following week.

'All set?' Mum started up the car and we were off. Auntie Glow was having a final pre-wedding bash with her friends from the bakery and me and Mum had been invited too.

'I'm so excited!' I kicked off my school shoes and wriggled into my jeans.

'I just hope it stays dry,' said Mum, turning up the road into town.

I peered out of the window. It had been solidly sunny for six days, which was pretty normal for Sunny Bay, even in October. Sunny Bay, that's where I live – a large seaside town with a big sandy beach and two piers; an old Victorian one that's a bit wrecked, and a brand-new, amazing one, with loads of stalls and rides, which is where we were heading now.

'There they are!' I shouted, as we drove into the car park.

Auntie Glow and her friends were sitting on a bench on the sea front, eating candyfloss and waving like crazy. We parked and went to join them.

'Wow! That's a great outfit!' I said.

Auntie Glow blushed scarlet. Her mates had dressed her in a (hen-night style) Halloween vampire costume, complete with fangs and a big black cape. 'I feel very silly,' she giggled. 'I hope Gordon doesn't see me!'

Gordon didn't work in the supermarket on Fridays. He helped out in the Sunny Bay museum instead. That was his real passion – history. He'd been doing an Open University history degree for the past four years – studying in between supermarket shifts – and one day he hoped to become a museum curator. Meanwhile, he spent his free time helping out in our little town museum, which was stuffed inside a modern building at the head of the pier.

'We'll sneak past so he won't spot you!' giggled Mum.

But Gordon *did* spot us. In fact he was waiting for

us, standing outside the museum with a gloomy look on his face.

'Gloria, I need to talk to you,' he said solemnly, and I felt a slight chill pass over me, as though a dark cloud had covered the sun.

'You girls go on ahead,' smiled Auntie Glow. 'I'll catch you up at the Little House of Horrors.'

That was the name of the newest attraction on the pier; an amazing haunted house ride, which you travelled round on a little ghost train. It was actually pretty scary! I'd been on it once and I kept my eyes shut the whole time. But Megan – my best mate, who's much braver than me – told me that she'd seen real ghosts floating round the dark rooms – a mad axeman, a weeping bride and a bunch of spooky circus performers . . . This time I promised myself I was going to keep my eyes open!

We stood outside the ride, watching the little ghost trains come and go, waiting for Auntie Glow for more than half an hour. But she didn't appear.

'Do you think everything's okay?' I asked Mum.

'Of course! Gordon's probably just got a case of wedding nerves. It's very common. Your dad was terrified before our wedding.'

But another twenty minutes went past and there was still no Auntie Glow. The girls from the bakery began to get restless, so Mum suggested we go on the ride. 'And if Gloria's still not here afterwards, we'll go and get a cuppa,' she added.

We paid our money and climbed on board. As we disappeared into the darkness I clutched Mum's hand. I know it's all make-believe, but it was super spooky all the same.

Straight away I felt something tickle my face – a spider's web, maybe – and despite my promise to myself, I covered my eyes. The sound of screaming started, high-pitched and freaky, and the train suddenly veered off to the right. I peeked out and gasped as a skeleton jangled horribly in front of me. Then the train turned sharply to the left and hurtled through another door into what looked like a dungeon. A row of spooky heads on spikes greeted us, winking and blinking and groaning horribly. Behind them three grisly bodies writhed on the wall, their arms and legs manacled together. As we went past, a hooded figure stepped out from the gloom with a huge bloody axe. 'Who's next?' he growled.

I gasped and grabbed on to Mum. 'It's just pretend!' she giggled. Then the train took off again, hurtling through some double doors into an old-fashioned circus ring that was lit up by a circle of burning torches. Our train trundled through the middle. At first it looked like no one was in there. Then there was a frightful wailing and some creepy laughter and a few big balls of white light bounced into the middle of the ring and turned into people – ghastly looking ghosts with green faces and long arms. Two of them were tumblers and the smallest one was a freaky young juggler who was spinning skulls on his fingertips. As I watched, the juggler glared at me menacingly and then a horrible thing happened – his eyeballs popped out!

'Aaaargh!' I screamed, and the ghost grinned, reminding me quite a lot of my brother Andy. The tumblers meanwhile were spinning wildly round the ring in opposite directions.

'They're going to crash,' I whispered to Mum.

And they did. Suddenly there was a jumble of body parts, until eventually they pulled themselves together, but now they both had the wrong bits. One had three legs, the other had too many arms and both had the wrong heads. But that didn't stop them taking off again, tumbling away wildly once more.

It was the weirdest show I'd ever seen. But it wasn't over yet. Just then there was a slight sigh from above and a beautiful young woman with long, silvery hair dropped down, balancing on a trapeze. She slipped as though about to fall, before catching the bar with one hand and spinning gracefully round and round. She began to go faster and faster, until suddenly she caught fire. I gasped and she let out a blood-curdling scream, then vanished altogether, leaving nothing but a few puffs of smoke.

Our train hurtled off again through a science laboratory with strange looking body parts stuffed inside jars – eyes that winked, a mouth that made kissy noises and a wiggly hand that waved at us. After that we entered a graveyard where ghouls began to rise slowly out of the graves, reaching out to grab at us.

The train took off just in time and suddenly we were inside a church and a bloodstained bride was thrashing around in the middle yelling, 'My dress is ruined! My dress is ruined!' And then a bell began to toll above us, the bride screamed and we tore through a final set of black doors. At last we were outside again in the lovely fresh air.

'Wow!' I heard one of the bakery girls say. 'That was so real! Shall we do it again?'

But I didn't want to. I was glad the nightmare was over.

Except it wasn't. Because standing there, waiting for us, was a sight more horrible than anything we'd seen on the ride. It was Auntie Gloria. But she no longer was the beautiful blooming bride-to-be. She now was a howling-her-head-off horrible banshee.

CHAPTER 3

'The wedding's off! Gordon's dumped me!'

We were sitting in the Blue Dolphin café at the end of the pier with steaming mugs of hot chocolate in front of us. The bakery girls had gone home and Mum had finally got Auntie Glow to stop crying long enough to explain what had happened.

'He says he can't face the fuss tomorrow,' she wailed, burying her face in her arms. 'The church, the guests the horse and carriage . . .' And then she started crying again.

'Oh, Glow, he doesn't mean it,' soothed Mum, stroking her sister's hand. 'He's just nervous, that's all. He'll change his mind, I'm sure of it.'

'He won't. He says he's not getting married. And he's going off on our honeymoon by himself.'

'What?' It was my turn to look shocked. That didn't sound fair.

'He says he needs time to *find himself*,' cried Auntie Glow. 'Without me!'

I felt a knot of crossness forming in my tummy. How could he? How could Gordon Twigg ruin everything? After all, it wasn't just Auntie Gloria's life he was ruining. It was mine too. 'What am I going to tell the kids at school?' I blurted without thinking. 'I've been going on about the wedding for weeks.'

Mum and Gloria looked at me, horrified. And then I realised how selfish I sounded.

'Sorry,' I muttered, my cheeks burning. 'I didn't mean to say that.' But inside I was seething. I wanted to go and find Gordon and tell him what I thought of him, right that minute. But Mum and Gloria were getting up to go.

'Don't worry,' Mum was saying, squeezing Auntie Glow's shoulders. 'Me and Jessie will take care of everything. We'll talk to the vicar and cancel the hotel. Everything will be all right. And maybe in a few weeks time Gordon will come to his senses.'

'If he survives that long,' I muttered to myself

through gritted teeth. I should probably tell you, I've got a bit of a temper. Dad calls me a firecracker because when I get really cross I explode! And I definitely felt ready to explode now.

But as we stepped out of the café, I shivered. The afternoon had gone and with it the sun. The night was sweeping in fast and there was a stiff coldness in the air I hadn't felt for ages. I zipped up my jacket and a heavy splodge of rain landed on my upturned face. Except it wasn't rain, it was hail. At first just a few small stones and then suddenly, as though someone had turned on a machine gun, it hammered down on our heads.

'Run for it!' I yelled, hailstones stinging my cheeks.

We made a mad dash down the pier, dodging people and pushchairs and puddles of slush that were already forming. As we hurtled past the museum, I glanced through the window hoping to spot Gordon. But he'd gone, which was maybe just as well. The wild weather wasn't making my bad mood any better!

'So let me get this right . . . I don't have to wear my suit?'

It was an hour later and me and Mum had dropped off Auntie Glow (still sobbing) and were back at home about to start ringing round and cancelling everything.

Andy, who never likes dressing up for anything, couldn't believe his luck when he heard the news. He punched the air with joy. 'No suit! RESULT!'

I glowered at him across the dining table. Mum frowned. 'Stop being so insensitive. Auntie Gloria's devastated,' she said.

Andy shrugged. 'Sorry, but I'm on Gordon's side. Who'd want to spend all day hanging around with a bunch of silly women in frilly frocks making a big fat fuss about flowers and hats and stuff. Yuck! I'm *never* going to get married!'

I gritted my teeth. 'No girl would have you.'

Andy smirked. 'Just because you won't get to dress up like a marshmallow, don't take it out on me.'

'Shut up!'

'Enough!' Mum banged her coffee cup on the table. 'Andy, if you've finished your dinner, you can go and do your homework. Jessie, I need your help. Can you remember the name of the girl at the florists?'

'Carol,' I said glumly. I knew her phone number

too. And the hotel manager's. And the vicar's. And the bloke's who'd been booked to drive Auntie Glow's horse and carriage. I knew them all.

'Right,' sighed Mum. 'I'd better make a start then.' And she headed off to the phone, leaving me alone with my misery. I mean, not only was the wedding off, but it was Halloween too, and all my mates were out trick or treating. I'd told them I was far too busy to join in but now I was stuck at home with nothing to do. Worse, come Monday morning when I went back to school, I'd have to tell everyone that I hadn't been a bridesmaid after all. I felt my face go red at the thought. 'It's just not fair,' I growled for the millionth time. And it wasn't. There I was with a fab bridesmaid's frock (and matching shoes) and a head full of wedding know-how, with nowhere to use it . . .

I picked up the local paper to distract myself. But it didn't work. Right in the middle was a double-page spread all about how to plan the perfect wedding with adverts for dress shops and photographers and Carol the florist. I quickly turned the page. And then I saw something that made me stop. And stare. And think. It was a tiny advert . . .

EXPERIENCED GARDENER FOR HIRE.
HAS OWN TOOLS AND LAWNMOWER.
CALL STEVE ON 719870 FOR A FREE QUOTE.

From somewhere in the deepest darkest corner of my brain an idea was shouting to be heard. I read the advert again. *Experienced gardener for hire.* And then it came to me – if gardeners could hire themselves out, then why not bridesmaids? Why shouldn't I make my own advert? I could picture it now:

Bridesmaid for hire. Has posh frock and shoes and loads of wedding know-how. Contact Jessie Pocket for a free quote.

I immediately threw down the paper and raced upstairs. I pushed all the stuff off my desk, grabbed some paper and pens, and settled down to write my advert. And then I stopped and realised that actually making and placing an advert would take ages. I'd have to post it off and wait for the newspaper to print it. And I'd probably have to pay for it too. I wanted to be a bridesmaid *now*, or tomorrow, or at the very latest, Sunday. An advert would take ages to work.

But a poster wouldn't. I could put a few of them up around town tonight. Maybe there was a bride out there right now who'd just been let down – perhaps her bridesmaid had broken her leg or got a bad bout of flu leaving the poor bride without. All I had to do was find her!

(Yeah, yeah, I know it sounds mad. But at the time, I wasn't thinking straight. And anyway, I'm an action girl – a doer not a thinker!) So I spent the next hour or so working my socks off. Luckily I had a good idea how to go about it. We'd done something similar in school last term, when we'd had to invent a business and make an advert for it. So I knew they had to be big and bold. Eye-catching but clear. With all the information a customer could need. So this is what I drew:

Yep. A picture of me in my bridesmaid's frock, pointing out the cool shoes, the hair accessory and explaining that I had loads of wedding knowledge and bags of bridesmaidy experience. (Okay, that last bit was a fib, but I was desperate.) I finished it off with my address and telephone number. I don't like to brag but actually it was pretty good, so I started on a second one, and then a third. I was just putting the finishing touches to a fourth poster when I heard a noise and Andy's head appeared around the door.

'What are you doing?'

'None of your business!' I growled.

But he was too quick for me. He darted in and grabbed the poster off my desk.

'Bridesmaid for hire?' he read. 'Ha! How desperate are you!'

'Give it back.' I tried to snatch the paper, but he held it high above my reach.

'This is the most stupid thing I've ever seen,' he said, shaking his head in mock horror. 'Were you really planning to put this up somewhere?'

I gritted my teeth and tried to reach the paper again.

'No way,' he said, shaking his head and holding it higher. 'Haven't you ever heard of stranger danger? Think of all the nutters out there. Mum will go mad when she sees this!'

'Give it back,' I howled. And then I did a bad thing. I kicked him in the shins. Hard!

'Ow! You little freak!' His face turned purple and I knew he was about to thump me, when suddenly he had a better idea. He grabbed the other bits of paper from my desk, raced over to the window and flung it open. Then he held up the posters, ripped them to shreds and chucked all the pieces outside.

I screamed and ran at him, in rage. But as usual he easily dodged past me before escaping into the hall. I heard him howling with laughter as he headed back to his room. I can honestly say I hated Andy right then. And I'd have swapped him for a half-sucked sweet.

I peered out into the darkness, wondering whether it was worth nipping out to look for the bits – maybe I could stick them back together? But then I noticed the rain and I realised the paper would be mush by now. For a moment I felt a tidal wave of tears bubbling up in my belly. But I didn't want Andy to hear me blub. So I swallowed them down and decided to go to bed instead.

When I was little and having trouble settling in at school, Mum used to tell me about 'morning magic'. She'd tuck me in at night and say, 'Don't worry, Jess, everything will look better in the morning.' And she was usually right. So I had one final glance at my bridesmaid's frock hanging all shiny and beautiful on my wardrobe door, and then (still refusing to cry) turned off the light, pulled the duvet over my head and hoped 'morning magic' still worked on ten-year-olds. But I never found out, because they came just before midnight.

CHAPTER 4

It had taken me ages to fall asleep, but after a lot of tossing and turning I'd finally drifted off. Unfortunately it didn't last long. A sudden noise made me stir. It sounded like a chuckle, low and sneaky. A lot like Andy. I opened one sleepy eye and saw a shadow by the door and presumed my brother had come back to gloat about the posters. So I reached out of bed and felt for one of my slippers. Then before he could move, I flung it at him. 'Get lost, Andy!' I mumbled. But I must have missed because the slipper hit the wall.

'Bad shot!' came a voice that wasn't Andy's. And then I heard a girl's voice, softer and silky, telling the first voice to 'hush'.

I gasped. Who were they? Burglars? Kidnappers?

Any minute I expected to feel a hand clamped over my mouth, before being bundled into a bag and whisked off into the night. Really I should have screamed. But I didn't. And then I heard the girl's voice again, from the other side of my room now . . .

'Oh,' she said. 'This must be the dress. It's a shame about the colour.'

'Yeah, it's gruesome,' said the other voice. 'So pink!'

And then I realised they could only be talking about one thing. My bridesmaid's dress. Something came over me then, wedding madness, maybe. I flicked on my bedside lamp, leapt out of bed and roared, 'It's not pink, it's rose!'

And then I gasped. Because it was *them* – the ghastly circus performers from the haunted house ride on the pier. Honestly, it was. I recognised them immediately. All four of them – the girl who turned to fire, with her silky silvery hair, the two freaky tumblers, who'd got their legs and heads muddled-up, and the smaller one who juggled the skulls.

I closed my eyes. This was obviously a nightmare. The worst kind – a dream within a dream! The type of nightmare that looks utterly real but could never possibly be. So I pinched myself. Quite hard. But when I opened my eyes they were still there. So I did it again, even harder this time.

'Why are you doing that?' asked the girl. 'You'll make your skin sore.'

And then it hit me. Like a shovel in the face. This wasn't a dream. This was *real*. The ghosts from the show were now standing in my bedroom. And that's when I screamed, or would have done, if a hand hadn't instantly clamped itself tightly over my mouth.

'Shut up,' said skull-boy, scowling down at me. 'You'll wake the dead!' Then he started to chuckle as though he'd just cracked a really funny joke. And the two tumblers joined in.

'Gerrr-off!' I mumbled from underneath skull-boy's hand. And I tried to bite him. But he just clamped harder.

'Let go of her, Charlie,' said the girl, slapping his hand away. 'You're so rude! It's no wonder she's scared. We've woken her up, trampled through her room, and haven't even introduced ourselves yet.'

Charlie rolled his eyes. And then reluctantly removed his hand. I was about to let rip when I saw something familiar in the girl's hand. *One of my posters.* Not in bits any more, but strangely whole again.

'But how . . . ?' I began.

The girl smiled. 'My name is Lena and these are my brothers – Tony, Albert and Charlie. And if you're Jessie Pocket, then I'd very much like to hire you.'

'What?' I felt like a bouncy castle that had been stabbed with a high-heeled shoe. All the air was suddenly sucked out of me and I had to fight to catch a breath.

'I'm a bride, you see,' said the girl, her white face turning ever so slightly pink. 'Or I shall be shortly, if you'll help me.'

'But who are you?'

'We're the Flying Leap-a-leenies,' said one of the tumblers, with a deep bow.

'The finest acrobats ever to have lived . . .' said the other.

'. . . or died!' added the first. 'If only your bedroom was bigger, we could show you.'

My mouth hung open like a goldfish.

'But there's no time,' said Lena gently. 'Perhaps later . . .'

I couldn't stop staring at them. Four white-faced figures, oddly see-through, like . . . ghosts, I suppose. And then suddenly all of them were looking at me.

'Er . . . when are you getting married?' I squeaked.

'Soon . . . a little after midnight,' Lena said vaguely.

I glanced at my clock. 11.05. 'But that's not long!'

Lena nodded. 'Yes, but there's always a bit more time on Halloween, don't you find?'

I frowned. 'Er . . . well . . .'

Skull-boy scowled at me. 'I told you she wouldn't understand.'

Lena ignored him. 'Every thirteenth All Hallow's eve, there's a thirteenth hour,' she said solemnly.

'Really?'

'Yes, and our kind always marry on the chime of the thirteenth hour. It's unlucky not to. Tonight is my wedding night, but I've lost my bridesmaid and I've been trying to find a replacement. Then Charlie spotted your poster.'

'But how? My brother tore it to bits.'

Lena's eyes sparkled. 'Anything is possible if you want it badly enough, especially on the night of the lucky thirteenth.'

I frowned. I was sure the number thirteen was supposed to be *un*lucky, but I didn't like to mention it.

Lena glanced at her watch – a little silver one with an old-fashioned face and a single hand. 'But we must go. If we don't, *he* might stop us.'

'Who?'

'I'll explain later. But for now, just say you'll help me?' She smiled and her whole face lit up like the moon. Then I knew I'd do anything to help her.

'Yes,' I whispered.

'Thank you.' She kissed my cheek and I shivered. It was like being touched by an icicle.

'Well, I'm not carrying that hideous dress!' said Charlie folding his arms. He reminded me so much of Andy, I felt like kicking him!

'I'll carry Jessie's dress,' said Lena firmly. 'And Tony, will you fly with her?'

'Fly?' I gasped.

'It's much faster.' Lena glanced at her watch again, looking flustered now. 'And I'm so terribly late . . . I still have to collect my dress, and then there's the cake, and the flowers . . . and . . .'

And instantly my bridesmaid know-how kicked in:

Rule Number 1. A bridesmaid must never let the bride get stressed.

'Don't worry, I'll sort that out,' I said, as though planning a ghostly wedding was something I knew all about. 'And hey, the flying thing sounds fine; I've been on a plane. How bad can it be?'

Charlie sniggered. But Lena dug her elbow into his side. 'Thank you,' she said. 'I knew you'd help, though perhaps you should wear some shoes,' she glanced at my bare feet.

As I slipped my wedding shoes out of their box, one of the tumblers peered at me.

'Did you say your name is Jessie Pocket?'

I nodded.

'Not any relation of Arthur Pocket, by any chance?'

'Who?'

'Arthur Pocket – the Pocket Rocket – the world's fastest human cannon ball! We used to work with him, many years ago . . .'

I shrugged. 'Don't think so.'

'You look very like him – same wild black hair and fiery eyes!'

I was about to tell him that my hair was not wild and my eyes were perfectly normal, thank you very much, but the other tumbler had already opened my bedroom door, letting in a blast of icy cold.

'Er . . . how did you get in here?' I asked. 'I suppose you just walked through the wall?'

But he didn't reply. He scooped me off my feet, and posted me through the window like a letter. I dropped like a stone. For one awful moment I thought I was about to go splat! when suddenly I felt a pair of ice-cold arms catch me and spin me and suddenly I was rising upwards like a rocket-propelled ballerina.

Tony grinned at me, over my shoulder. 'Ta dah! See, told you we are great acrobats!' And just to prove the point, he then did an airborne roly-poly. As the ground rushed towards me once more, I very nearly barfed. But I managed to say, 'Great!' through gritted teeth. Then I shut my eyes and vowed not to open them again until the wind stopped whistling around my ears.

CHAPTER 5

Thankfully it had stopped raining. But it was really cold. I was only wearing my PJs, and though they were the cosy ones I got last Christmas, they didn't keep any of the October chill out. I don't think we were up there long, and we weren't very high (I had one tiny peek and saw the top of a tree brush my shoes). But by the time we landed, my nose and hands felt blue and my teeth were chattering like crazy.

We'd arrived in a dark street surrounded by high buildings. There were cardboard boxes and bags of rubbish lying around and I noticed other creatures of the night scuttling past – cats and . . . rats! I grimaced. The only light was from Tony's skin, which was bright white now. It was a bit like having a human torch, except he wasn't human.

'Where are we?'

'The dress shop,' smiled Tony.

And then the others appeared.

'Are you okay?' Lena asked, landing next to me, her face creased with concern.

I nodded, still trying to stop my teeth from chattering.

'It's just in here . . .' Lena said, leading me towards a door, which opened as she approached. A flight of steps disappeared down and Lena led the way, her skin now as bright as her brother's. The boys didn't follow.

'Girls' stuff,' Lena giggled. 'By the way, you'll meet my fiancé Freddie a bit later. He's such a sweetheart. I'm sure you'll like him.'

And then another door at the bottom of the stairs opened, spilling a red glow into the stairwell, and a voice called a greeting from within. I blinked in the light. Inside sat a young woman behind a sewing machine, close to an open fire, which was crackling with green flames. The woman's dark hair was plaited to her waist. Her cheeks were round and rosy like apples and her lips were red, the same colour as the walls and the floor, or at least what I could see of it. Much of the room was hidden under mountains of dresses. They were everywhere. Purple, gold, red of course. But mostly black and green. As I looked around, there was a sudden fluttering of wings and a dark shadow swooped over our heads, cawing loudly. I ducked.

'He won't hurt you,' smiled the woman, catching a small crow on her hand. 'It's just that he's scared of pink. It's not a colour he sees much of in here.'

I glanced at my PJs (neon pink with bunnies on them) and at my bridesmaid's frock, which Lena was still carrying. 'That's not actually pink,' I said nodding to the dress. 'It's rose. And rose is very "in" for weddings this year!'

The seamstress made a face, but Lena coughed . . .

'This is Pallidia Black,' she told me. 'She's been making my wedding dress.' Then she turned to the seamstress. 'Pallidia, I'd like to introduce you to Jessie Pocket, my new bridesmaid . . .'

The seamstress raised an eyebrow and gave Lena a strange look, which I didn't understand.

'If Jessie doesn't mind,' Lena went on. 'I was

wondering if you could alter her dress a little, so we look similar.'

For a second I was appalled. How could she want to change my beautiful bridesmaid's frock? But then I remembered:

Rule Number 2. A bridesmaid must always fit in with her bride's colour scheme.

Maybe the flowers in Lena's bouquet were yellow or red, or something . . .

'Of course,' I said cheerfully. After all, it wasn't as though Auntie Glow cared any more.

The sewing lady took my dress with a frown. As she sat back down at her machine I heard her mutter, 'Pink, hideous pink!'

'It's *rose!*' I corrected crossly, under my breath.

Then Lena took my hand again and led me to the back of the room, where a burgundy screen stood next to a long mirror. 'I'll just go and change into my dress,' she said as she disappeared behind it. 'I won't be a minute.'

While I waited, I watched the sewing lady at the other end of the room. Her own frock was a strange purple, which seemed to shimmer as she worked.

I blinked. No, it wasn't purple, it was green . . . actually, no not green, more blue . . . or should that be orange. Yeah, burned orange. And then it changed again and became black with purple swirls. Looking at it made my head hurt. I closed my eyes, and when I opened them again the dress was red. Definitely red. Like blood. I shivered.

'Pallidia's a stitch witch, you know,' whispered Lena from behind the screen. 'Such clever fingers . . .'

A witch? Weren't they supposed to be old and warty? 'So, er . . . where are you getting married?' I asked, changing the subject.

I heard Lena sigh. 'At the fisher folk cemetery . . . you know, St Peter's churchyard, near the old pier on the sea front.'

'A graveyard?'

'Yes, though of course I wish it was my home plot. I always feel a bride should marry near her family tomb, don't you?'

'Er . . . well . . . yes, I suppose so.'

'And that was my plan – to marry in St Julian's graveyard, you know, up on the hill, where all us show folk are buried . . .'

I bit my lip. Of course I knew St Julian's church. That was where Auntie Glow was supposed to be getting married tomorrow!

'Then *he* found out,' said Lena, her voice quieter now. 'And ruined it all.'

'Who?'

But at that moment Lena stepped out from behind the screen. And she looked so lovely I forgot what we'd been talking about.

'What do you think?' she said, twirling round gracefully.

I was speechless. I'd never seen anything more beautiful. Her dress fell to the floor in a waterfall of finely spun silvery lace the same colour as her hair. And woven into the lace were little sparkles of deep purple that flashed and glinted when the light hit them.

'Could you help me with the veil?'

She handed me a feather-light piece of the same material, which had a silver comb fixed to one end. As she bent down, I carefully attached it to her hair. It was like threading thin air.

'That's it – perfect,' she said, straightening up.

I still couldn't speak. She was like a beautiful ice queen, escaped from a storybook.

'Splendid!' said the stitch witch, appearing silently by my side. 'Needle spiders make the most beautiful cobwebs, perfect for a wedding dress.'

'Cobwebs?'

'Yes, hand-sewn with beetle hearts!'

'Oh.'

'Now it's your turn, Jessie.' And the stitch witch handed me my frock.

Except it wasn't my frock. Not any more. The colour had changed. The rose pink had been replaced by a pale, icy purple. It was shorter too, with ragged, sharp cuts to the hem, and a thin satin gauze now covering the skirt. The lavender sash was covered with tiny pearls. And over the chest was the same cobweb lace as Lena's dress. As it moved,

I noticed the dress also had the same twinkling purpley bits . . . beetle hearts!

'You do like it, don't you?' asked Lena nervously.

'I love it!' I gasped. And I did.

The stitch witch sighed happily. 'Do you need help putting it on?'

I shook my head and stepped behind the screen. The dress felt chilly to touch, but as I slipped it on I didn't feel cold. I felt oddly warm. I looked in the mirror and a strange ghostly flower sprite stared back – it was me! My hair, which I'd been growing out for ever so that I could wear it pinned up for Auntie Glow's wedding, suddenly looked longer. And thicker. And blacker. It curled round my shoulders and snaked down my back like a serpent. It definitely didn't stick up all frizzy like it usually did. For a second I wondered if the stitch witch had fixed that too. I was just about to ask when suddenly I heard a boy's voice, urgent and anxious. I peeked round the screen and saw Charlie fly into the room.

'He's coming, Lena. You must go!'

'What?' Lena gasped. 'Here?'

'Yes – go now!' Charlie yelled, grabbing his sister's hand and pulling her towards the wall.

'But what about Jessie?' Lena glanced at me nervously.

'I'll protect her,' the stitch witch said.

Lena hesitated for a moment, then she and Charlie vanished.

'What's happening?' I yelped.

But the stitch witch pushed me back behind the screen. 'Stay there,' she hissed. 'Whatever happens, don't speak, don't move, don't breathe, if you can help it.' Then she pushed me down on to the floor, and began heaping dresses on top of me.

'What are you doing?' I yelled, my voice muffled by the layers of fabric now covering my head.

'Saving your life,' she whispered as more dresses crushed on top of me, and instinctively I curled into a ball, hoping the witch would remember I still needed to breathe. And then the room was silent. But not for long . . .

CHAPTER 6

There was a rushing of wind, like a tornado. And then an angry man's voice roared into the room . . .

'Where is she?' it boomed. 'I know Lena's been here! Where is she?'

'Get out!' I heard Pallidia shout. 'You don't scare me!'

Then I heard a terrified squawking, which I presumed was the stitch witch's crow, followed by a scream and then the squawking stopped. I bit my lip. I had no idea who was out there, but I felt terrified.

And then the voice dropped to a deep bullying growl. 'I told you what would happen if you helped her; if you disobeyed me!'

'I'm not scared of you, or your cameras,' replied Pallidia, though her voice was trembling now. 'They can't kill me.'

'No!' yelled the voice. 'But they can kill your customers. And they can make your head hurt so much you'll never be able to work again.'

Cameras? What cameras? What on earth were they talking about?

'Get out!' Pallidia yelled again.

But the intruder wasn't done yet.

'I know she's planning to marry him tonight. But she can't, see! Because I've got the graveyard surrounded. If she or anyone else tries to get in, they'll be dead. Deader than dead. Forever dead. Understand?'

'Just get out of here,' shouted the stitch witch again. 'Go on – shoo!'

But he wasn't listening. He was sniffing . . .

'I can smell human hair. Human skin. Human blood. A human heart is beating . . .' His voice was so close now I could almost feel flecks of spit. 'Come out, come out, wherever you are . . .'

But suddenly there was a loud *bang*! from the other end of the room, followed by several more. And the angry voice suddenly screamed, 'Spiders? No!'

Then there were more bangs And the room turned cold. Icy cold.

'You'll pay for this,' the voice threatened. And then suddenly he was gone.

I would have breathed a sigh of relief, except I couldn't, because my little pocket of air underneath the clothes seemed to have vanished with him. The coats on top of me felt heavier too, as though someone was sitting on them. I gasped for breath and felt a wave of tiredness wash over me. My eyes began to droop and then suddenly I heard a *crack*! and arms were reaching for me.

'Jess? Jess? Wake up . . .' I felt as though my eyes would never open again. Pallidia patted my cheeks, then I felt water splash on my face and I was alert again.

'What happened?' I looked around the room. It was no longer red. It was bright white, covered in thick layers of ice – cobweb ice, like Lena's dress. Even the fire had gone out and was iced over. I reached out and touched the floor. My fingers tingled. Then I saw something move in the far corner of the room, a large white spider about the size of my dad's fist. It was crystal clear, as though made of glass, and its feet made a horrible tinkle-tapping noise as it scuttled around the room.

Pallidia sighed. 'I thought I'd got them all.' Then she muttered something under her breath and the spider froze and turned to dust, *ice* dust!

'Needle spiders,' she shrugged. 'They make wonderful webs, so beautiful to sew. I didn't want to waste them on him, but I know how much he hates them, so I stuck a few spider eggs in the fire. They burst open like popcorn when you heat them up.' She looked around the room. 'Though it'll take a while to clean this up . . .'

'But who was he?'

'The Duke of Spooks,' said the witch, her lip curled. 'That's what he calls himself anyway.'

'But why was he here?'

The witch shrugged. She was searching around in the ice for something. 'He was looking for Lena. He doesn't want her to get married.'

'Why not?' I was desperately trying to understand, but my brain felt slow, weighed down by the coats and ice that had covered me.

'Because he wants her for himself,' said Pallidia. 'But also because she's escaped from his show . . .'

'The haunted house ride on the pier?'

The witch nodded. 'The duke owns the pier, and everything on it. Lena and her brothers and dozens of other ghosts have been imprisoned there; they have to work for the duke and do as he says or he'll kill them!'

I stared at her, horrified. 'How?' I didn't know a ghost could die – weren't they already dead?

Pallidia held up her hands like a camera and made a clicking noise, as though pressing the camera's button. 'Taking a photo kills a ghost, for ever. So he's put cameras everywhere to keep the ghosts in line. Haven't you noticed?'

I shook my head.

'There are CCTV cameras all over the pier. Every street in the centre of town has them too. The duke is a very rich and powerful man. He's also a town councillor and he's persuaded the rest of the councillors to pay for them. He says they're needed to prevent shoplifting and bad human behaviour, but really he's using them to control the ghosts. If they step out of line, he zaps them!'

'But isn't he a ghost himself?'

'No, he's much more powerful. He's a Gho-man. Half ghost, half human. He died last year when his car ran off a cliff near Middle Spit Sands. Except he didn't. Somehow those beastly paramedics managed to get his heart started again. And now he's neither dead nor alive.'

'And that's a bad thing?'

'It is for the ghosts in this town. He has all their ghostly powers – he can walk through walls, he has powerful hearing and powerful eyesight, he can fly and disappear. But he looks human, he still has a heartbeat and, worst of all,' the stitch witch sighed, 'cameras don't hurt him.'

'Or you?'

She shook her head. 'They can't kill witches. But they do give us ferocious headaches. Mega-migraines!'

She bent down and lifted something from the icy floor. It was her little crow, limp and lifeless. Except it wasn't a crow any more . . . I looked closer and realised it was a reptile – a small lizard, maybe.

Pallidia smiled sadly. 'Brimstone wasn't really a crow, he was a shape-shifting Antarctic chameleon; a creature that could change into anything."

I didn't like the way she talked about him in the past tense. I bit my lip. 'Did he kill him?'

She nodded. 'The duke never goes anywhere without a camera.'

'So he was a ghost?'

'Sort of. Not a spirit like Lena, but a zombie animal. He died once before, but a friend brought him back for me.'

'Maybe your friend could do it again.'

'Maybe.' The witch slipped the crow into her pocket. Then she glanced at her watch. 'You must go. Lena will be looking for you.'

But I still had so many questions. 'I don't understand – how can Lena get married if the duke knows about the wedding? He said he had the cemetery surrounded. Won't she be in danger?'

The stitch witch smiled mischievously. 'Lena's cleverer than he is. The duke thinks she's getting married in the old cemetery on the hill – the one where all the show folk are buried. But Lena's moved the venue to St Peter's down by the pier! That's why everything is so last-minute.'

And then a thought popped into my head. 'What happened to Lena's last bridesmaid?'

Pallidia shrugged. Then she ran her finger across her throat and a shiver passed down my spine.

'Killed,' I whispered. 'By the Duke of Spooks?'

The witch nodded sadly.

CHAPTER 7

As I walked up the stairs and out on to the street, I wondered what my fate might be if I carried on being Lena's bridesmaid.

Well at least he can't zap me with a camera, I reminded myself, though I didn't like to think how he might dispose of his human enemies.

'You took your time,' came a voice from the dark.

I jumped. It was Charlie – skull-boy – leaning against the wall, drumming his fingers impatiently. For the first time I had a good look at him. Although his annoying manner reminded me of Andy, he didn't look much like him. My brother is tall and fair, like my dad, whereas Charlie was short and wiry and despite his all over ghostly grey-white colour I reckoned his hair had probably once been as dark as mine.

'Are you ready then?'

'Yeah,' I shrugged. 'But we don't need to fly, do we?'

He rolled his eyes. 'It's faster than walking!'

'I like slow!'

'Suit yourself!'

He didn't walk, of course. He floated along in front of me. But I reckon he only did it to make himself look taller.

'How old are you, anyway?' I asked. We looked about the same age, though I was definitely more mature.

'I was born in 1902,' he said, 'which means I'm centuries older than you, so I'm in charge!'

'Not centuries,' I snapped. But all the same, I couldn't really argue.

I followed him in silence and as we turned the corner, I realised we were at the far end of Sunny Bay, a few streets away from the sea front and the old tumbledown Victorian pier – the Grand pier – which was pretty wrecked and had been closed to the public for longer than I'd been alive.

As we crossed a street, Charlie suddenly crashed down next to me and pushed me hard against a wall, dropping back into the shadows himself. Straight away, I could see why. High above us, across the road, fixed to a tall metal post was a rotating camera, which was now pointing directly at us. I spotted several more as I looked around. Strange, I went shopping with my mum every Saturday but I'd never noticed the cameras before. Now their beady metal eyes gave me the creeps.

'Okay,' said Charlie as the camera's head began to turn away. 'Let's go. We'll collect the cake on the way.' Then he took my hand and we ran (well, he floated) quickly down the street and round the corner into a dark alley. He let go of me and made himself brighter so I could see. 'Come on,' he snapped. 'It'll be dawn by the time we get to the graveyard.'

Charlie floated down the alley for a bit, and then disappeared through a wall, leaving me in darkness.

'Hey,' I yelled. 'I don't do walls, remember!'

Charlie's head reappeared for a second. 'There's a door, you silly still-alive!' Then he was gone, and I had to feel for the door with my hands. By the time I'd found the handle and opened it, I was ready to thump him. But I didn't get the chance because suddenly I

found myself inside a busy baker's shop. I couldn't
see Charlie but there were loads of others – all ghosts,
I presumed, most quite ordinary looking, carrying
shopping baskets and bags. A woman in a white apron
and cap was serving behind the counter, handing out
ghostly loaves of bread and parcelling up pretty little
see-through cakes.

'What a lovely dress,' said an old lady next to me.

I glanced down. I'd forgotten I was wearing my
bridesmaid's frock. 'Er . . . thanks,' I said.

'Going to a wedding?'

I nodded.

'Is it lovely Lena's wedding, by any chance?'

I nodded again.

'I must come along for a look . . .' Her grey eyes twinkled. 'Such a beauty, that one. Up at St Julian's cemetery, I suppose.'

I shook my head, and without thinking said, 'No, St Peter's – down by the old pier.'

'Really? Are you sure?' The old lady looked puzzled for a moment.

And then I remembered it was supposed to be a secret. I was just about to correct myself when Charlie reappeared with a giant cake box. I wondered if I should tell him what I'd just done, but I didn't get the chance.

'Come on,' he grumbled. 'We need to move faster. If only you could fly!'

I scrambled after him. By the time I'd opened the door, he was through the wall and halfway down the alley so I had to run to catch up with him, which wasn't easy in my bridesmaid's shoes.

'Are there loads of your kind in Sunny Bay?' I called, hoping he'd slow down to reply.

Charlie shrugged. 'Loads of people come here to retire and eventually they all pop off, so of course there are loads of ghosts.'

'Then why haven't I seen any?'

'Maybe you don't look hard enough,' he snapped. Then he stopped and turned to face me. 'Look, the truth is, we ghosts don't hang about as much as we used to. We can't. If we do, we get zapped. Or locked up in his show. The only safe place for us since the duke arrived is in our graves. And who wants to spend all day stuck inside a tomb? It's boring, boring, boring. But that's death, I suppose. Now, come on . . .'

We were close to the sea front now. I could smell the salt in the air and the heavy stink of fish. And then suddenly we were out in the open and the beach lay in front of us, like a huge golden puddle. The tide was far out and the sand seemed to sparkle in the moonlight. Charlie nodded to the crumbling old Victorian pier that stood nearby. 'That's where we used to perform, in the big theatre at the end – The Grand they called it.' He stopped floating for a moment and looked longingly at the far end of the pier, where nothing now remained of the theatre.

'There were loads of us back then, all show folk – acrobats, horse riders, Tammy with her tigers and old Arthur, the human cannon ball . . .'

I looked at the pier and wondered what it had looked like in Charlie's day. It was difficult to imagine. Now it just lurked in the bay like an old pile of dinosaur bones. 'What happened to it?' I asked.

Charlie shrugged. 'It had been falling apart for years, but no one bothered to repair it. Then finally fire took it, and we all know who dropped the match.' Charlie's face suddenly looked fierce, but then he sighed. 'We were dead long before the fire, of course.'

'Er . . . how did you . . . erm . . . well, you know . . .'

Charlie grinned impishly. 'You mean how did we die? The rope split. We were doing our famous family balancing trick – the Great Leap-a-leenies – up on the high wire without a safety net. All four of us balancing on each other's shoulders, when suddenly the rope broke, we hit the deck and broke our necks. Then we stopped being the Great Leap-a-leenies and became the Scary Creep-a-leenies.' As he spoke, Charlie swivelled his head all the way round like an owl, and then his eyeballs popped out!

I screamed. I couldn't help myself. And Charlie howled with laughter.

I gritted my teeth. 'You act like a four year old!'

Charlie stopped laughing, shoved his eyes back into their sockets and puffed out his cheeks. 'Girls,' he muttered. 'No sense of humour!'

I was trying to think of a cutting reply, but he'd already turned away, heading for a tumbledown old building across the road. I read the sign on its wall: St Peter's Chapel and Fishermen's Mission. And then I realised Charlie had vanished altogether – straight through the wall as usual – leaving me in the dark to find the door . . .

'Jess!' Lena was suddenly by my side. 'Thank goodness you're safe.' And then she saw how cross I looked. 'I hope Charlie hasn't been teasing you. He doesn't mean it. He just misses being alive sometimes.' She squeezed my hand. 'Come inside, we're tying to sort everything out. The vicar has arrived, but Freddie hasn't. He's gone to find our guests. Lots of them have got lost. Then there's the band. They're here, but they don't know where to sit. Everything's in such a terrible muddle.'

And suddenly I forgot she was a ghost. And that it was the middle of the night. And I'd just been seriously spooked by the Duke of Spooks. 'Don't worry,' I said, following her inside the chapel. 'I'll sort it all out.'

And together we began to straighten out the mess. Lena meanwhile, insisted I wear her watch, so I could see how much time we had before thirteen o'clock. There were no numbers on it, just little marks that counted down towards the thirteenth hour. As I watched it, I began to feel as flustered as Lena. But then I pulled myself together and got stuck in. There was plenty to do.

The graveyard was a small rectangle with tall gloomy trees on three sides, and the chapel wall making up the fourth, with a large clock on its tower. Many of the headstones had fallen down and everything was covered in ivy. In the middle was a grassy dome. The plague mound, Lena told me cheerfully. That was where she and Freddie would get married, while the guests sat or stood around amongst the headstones.

As I looked around I noticed several ghostly shadows emerging from the graves. The dead fisher folk, I reckoned, peeking out to see what all the noise was about. I took a deep breath and tried not to stare.

My first job was to find a place for the band. They were a ghastly bunch – foul old zombies with fallen-in faces and a bit of an odour problem, who played instruments made of bones and spent a lot of time tuning them, which sounded like someone being strangled.

Then there was the wedding breakfast to arrange. Tony and Albert, who'd been stringing fairy-light skulls around the walls, suggested we use some flat headstones at the back to lay out the food. I tried not to look at the names on the graves as I clambered among them, putting up candles and little wind chimes that tinkled in the breeze.

Tony grinned at me as I carefully avoided standing on one especially large headstone.

'He won't mind, you know.'

I made a face. 'Do you know him?'

Tony glanced at the name. 'No. But maybe he's not a ghost. Not everyone becomes one, some people are just dead.'

'Really?'

He nodded. 'Our parents aren't ghosts. We're not sure why. Perhaps it's down to how tired you are when you pop off. Some people just want to put their feet up, while others just aren't ready to rest in peace!' As he spoke he flipped over and did a somersault.

'How do you do that?'

In reply, he did a triple cartwheel.

I sighed. 'I'm rubbish at gymnastics. You should see me in PE.'

'Perhaps you're just trying too hard.'

'What do you mean?'

'Don't think about it. Just do it!' And he cartwheeled over and over again, landing in a one-handed headstand. 'Just do what comes natural,' he chuckled.

'I don't think that would work for me.'

Tony flipped upright again. 'If you throw a ball at someone, they'll catch it, won't they?' To prove the point, he scooped up a fallen crab apple and hurled it at me.

I ducked.

'Well, most people will catch it.' He grinned. 'But acrobats don't just catch balls, we catch people too.' As he spoke there was a *whoosh*! of air and his brother

Albert somersaulted on to his shoulders. Without turning round, Tony caught him easily. 'See! If you throw a person at an acrobat, they'll catch them!'

'Don't you ever have an off day and drop each other?'

But before Tony could answer, Lena gave a sudden cry from the other end of the churchyard. And he and Albert flew towards her.

CHAPTER 8

I raced after them, not bothering about whose head I was treading on. I could see Lena sitting at the other end of the graveyard, silvery tears streaking down her cheeks.

'Oh, Jess, it's a disaster,' she wept. 'I've forgotten my parents' wedding rings.'

Charlie scuffed the ground with his see-through shoes. 'It's my fault. I left them in the family vault.'

'Up at the other cemetery?' I asked.

He nodded, miserably.

'Can't someone just go and get them.' I glanced at Lena's watch. 'There's still time.'

She shook her head. '*He's* there, waiting for us.'

The Duke of Spooks – of course! How could I have forgotten about him?

'But *I* can go,' I said. 'Cameras can't hurt me.'

'It's too dangerous,' said Lena. 'You don't know what he's capable of.'

'But if someone could just fly me up there,' (I couldn't believe I was actually suggesting another crazy night flight) 'then I can sneak in, get the rings and be back here before you know it.'

'I'll take her,' said Charlie. 'After all, it was me who forgot the rings.'

'But the cameras,' said Lena, putting her arm around her little brother. 'No, I don't want either of you risking your lives. We'll do without them,' she said bravely. After a moment she gave a sad smile, then turned and walked away. Tony and Albert shrugged and moved off too. But Charlie stayed where he was, glaring up into the night sky, his hands balled into angry fists. 'He won't win!' he growled. 'I won't let him win. He's had us locked up in that silly show, making us do stupid stunts for silly tourists for months, and now he's stopping my sister from having our mother's wedding ring. It's not fair.'

I bit my lip, suddenly feeling guilty that I'd seen the show. 'Er . . . how did you get out of there anyway?'

'Freddie freed us. He's an escapologist – you know, like Harry Houdini, only better. He found a secret way out. And sprung us.'

'Is he a ghost too?'

'Yeah – but a free spirit. No one could keep Freddie in a box.'

'Maybe he could fetch the rings then?'

Charlie made a face, as though I was the biggest blockhead in the history of blockheads. Instantly I had the urge to kick him again, but I resisted.

'Freddie's busy,' he growled. 'He's gone to free the other ghosts from the haunted house ride, and to find the guests who've got lost.'

I nodded. With the last-minute change of venue it was going to take ages to round up all the lost souls currently wandering around Sunny Bay.

Charlie glanced over his shoulder and then lowered his voice. 'But I've made up my mind. I'm going to get the rings myself.'

'Then I'll come too.'

He glared at me, as though he thought I was teasing him. But I wasn't:

Rule Number 3. For good luck, a bride must

wear something old, something new, something borrowed and something blue.

Maybe the rings were Lena's borrowed thing, or her old one. Or maybe they just meant a lot to her. If Lena's mother couldn't come to her wedding, then the very least I could do was make sure she had her mother's ring.

Charlie frowned. 'It could be dangerous.'

'I'm not scared.'

'Okay then.' And he held out his hand to me.

I hesitated for a millisecond and then took it, and he led me away from the others, into the stillness of the dusty old chapel and then back out on to the sea front.

'Are you sure?' he said fiercely. 'Don't want to change your mind, silly still-alive?'

'Nope, dead-head, I don't!'

Charlie grinned and then spun me around, so I was facing away from him. He clamped his hands on my sides, and we took off like a rocket. I was the airborne ballerina again, firing up into the sky. This time I kept my eyes open and after a few terrifying moments I actually stopped wanting to throw up and started to like it. Love it, even. I was flying. Really flying. Like

Superman without the tights. (Though I wished I'd had the tights. It was freezing up there!)

We flew over streets and houses, and all the familiar stuff in Sunny Bay I'd seen a million times. But from the sky it looked totally different, all twinkly and pretty.

There was only one slightly hairy moment, when we took a short cut across the bay and I wondered if Charlie might drop me in the sea for a joke. I'm sure my brother would have done. But then I remembered how little time we had. By my reckoning, we had just over an hour before the clock chimed thirteen and Lena and Freddie must marry.

'Not far now,' Charlie whispered, his breath cold, like snow against my ear.

I glanced down and recognised the street we were flying over. It was Gordon Twigg's, and there was his house. If we hadn't been in such a hurry, I'd have asked Charlie to drop in and scare the socks off him!

Suddenly, we began to go down. And then I felt the ground under my feet again. Charlie pulled me into the shadows. His skin was no longer bright. He was a dark-grey colour and I could barely see him. 'There are two entrances to the cemetery,' he whispered. 'The main one is on the other side, but the back gate is just round the corner – that's where we'll try to get in. Remember, the duke will have watchers everywhere. We must be careful.'

'What sort of watchers?' My heart was racing

and suddenly I felt terrified at the thought of meeting the man whose booming voice I'd heard at Pallidia's shop.

'Hell hounds, probably. And ghouls. Anyone he can bully into helping him.' Charlie squeezed my hand. 'Are you sure you want to do this? You don't have to, you know. You could just go home. I'll take you and I'll understand.' For the first time there was not a hint of sarcasm in his voice. He actually meant it.

I nodded. 'I'm sure.'

But Charlie still looked doubtful. 'The duke's a bad man, you know. He killed Freddie!'

'How?'

'Freddie was starring in an escapology show on the Grand pier, long after we were dead, of course. We used to haunt the pier back then. And hang out in the roof of the theatre and watch the acts. One night Freddie stayed on after his show had ended to rehearse a new trick. Secretly I think he was hoping to spot Lena, as he'd seen her watching him before. But Freddie wasn't the only still-alive around that night. A local estate agent was there too, a man called Roger Pilkington-Smith. He set fire to the pier. He wanted to build a new one, you see – a better one – and make lots of money in the process. He didn't know Freddie was still in the theatre, of course. Not that he'd have cared if he did. Anyway, the fire spread quickly. We tried to rescue Freddie, but the smoke had already killed him.'

'That's awful.'

'Yeah, especially as Roger Pilkington-Smith got away with it. No one suspected him of course – such a well respected rich man.'

'And that was the Duke of Spooks, before he was a Gho-man?'

'Yep!'

Suddenly I didn't feel scared any more. I felt angry. 'Come on,' I said. 'I'm going to get those rings. And no murdering estate agent is going to stop me!'

Charlie grinned.

'But promise me that at the first sight of a camera you vanish, okay. I don't want Lena losing a brother tonight.'

Charlie nodded. And we moved quickly down the street, towards the gates of the graveyard.

CHAPTER 9

St Julian's cemetery was an altogether fancier affair than the fisher-folk churchyard of St Peter's. Of course I'd been there before. I'd visited the church with my family, and Auntie Glow and Gordon Twigg had held a wedding rehearsal there the weekend before. But I'd never noticed the graveyard. It was bigger and more open than St Peter's. And even the back gates were tall and smart looking, with beautiful designs carved into the railings.

We crouched in the shadows across the road, sheltering beneath three fat fir trees. Just as Charlie had predicted, there were a dozen or so watchers on patrol.

'Zombie ghouls,' he whispered. 'Very stupid. Like zombies but much slower.'

Slow or not, there was no mistaking the cameras strung around their necks.

Charlie leaned in closer. 'If I can make it past them and into the graveyard, I'll be safe. Cameras don't work on hallowed ground.'

'Maybe I could distract them?' I said. 'And while they're looking at me, you could slip past and get the rings.'

Charlie nodded. 'It's worth a try.'

I took a deep breath and stepped out of the shadows.

'Don't forget,' he hissed. 'Ghouls eat human flesh.'

Now he tells me. But it was too late to worry because one of them had already spotted me.

'Er . . . excuse me?' I said, walking nervously towards him. 'I seem to be lost. Can you tell me how to get to Windmill Avenue?'

The ghoul grunted and spat a blob of green gunge on the ground. Then he sniffed the air and smiled hungrily at me. It wasn't a pretty sight. Zombie ghouls are not the pretty boys of the underworld. Their faces are like runny candles. Their hair is slimy. And their bodies ooze with maggoty flesh-rot. There's also a distinct smell of dead-dog about them. I grimaced.

'Go on!' hissed Charlie from behind me. 'Get closer! But be careful!'

Closer, but be careful? I rolled my eyes. How was I supposed to do that?

The ghoul meanwhile was flexing his jaws, clanking his teeth together, little dribbles of drool dripping down his chin. I felt like a mouse with a cat about to pounce.

'Maybe I'll just try going this way,' I said pointing away from the gates, away from him.

I turned and started walking. And then I began to run. But several more watchers had seen me now and there was a sudden howl from another. And then two more began to growl. Others were sniffing the air, smacking their lips hungrily. I'm not a runner. I'm small and slightly clumsy, and my posh shoes didn't help. But even so, I took off like an Olympic athlete. There's nothing like a pack of ghouls on your tail to increase your speed. But I didn't get far.

The first ghoul outran me in seconds, grabbing my dress with his long yellow nails.

'Watch the frock,' I shouted, or I would have done if my throat hadn't jammed with terror. I tried to kick him, but my shoe just hit maggoty flesh and a gush of green yuck oozed out. I wanted to heave! Then the ghoul opened his mouth like a crocodile. God, his breath stank. I covered my nose with my hand and for a second I thought he was actually going to bite my head off like I was a giant jelly baby. But just then ghoul number two reached us and wrenched me away from his pal. Then ghoul number one tried to snatch me back and for a few minutes they were both tugging on my arms, like toddlers scrapping over a cuddly toy. Then the rest of the ghouls appeared and a fight broke out. It was an ugly affair; lots of groaning and moaning and leg and head pulling. Limbs began to fall off and a puddle of maggoty green slime appeared beneath them. But at least I was forgotten. I backed away slowly, keeping my eyes closely on them, in case they spotted me escaping. And then disaster. I reversed right into the Duke of Spooks himself. Bump! I turned and there he was. I knew it was him straight away. He towered over me like a bus shelter. Big and broad, with his hair flicked back in a bouncy bouffant style that probably took hours to achieve (with a massive hairdryer and a mega-can of hairspray to boot!).

'You,' he growled. For such a big, beefy bloke, he had tiny piggy eyes that glared at me wickedly from his full fat face. 'I smelled you before, at that witch's den. You should be at home, little girl, tucked up safe in bed, not prowling the streets looking for trouble!' And then he noticed my fancy frock and a slow, evil smile swept over his face. 'You're helping her, aren't you?' he spat. 'Lena!'

At the sound of her name, the ghouls stopped scrapping and started reaching for their cameras, which wasn't easy, seeing as loads of them had lost their arms by now. The few who could began taking photos of me. Click! Click! Clickety click!

The duke rolled his eyes in disgust 'She's human,' he growled. 'Not a ghost.'

But I'd already seized the chance to scarper. I was off like a flash, running towards the graveyard. I had to find Charlie. But the duke sprang up and was above and then in front of me in a heart beat. He grasped my arm tightly this time, his long, sharp nails biting into my flesh. I winced. It hurt!

'Going somewhere? Like a wedding maybe?'

I refused to answer, and he shook me until my teeth rattled. 'Where is she?' he screamed.

I glanced at the graveyard gates, and his eyes narrowed. 'Were you the distraction, so she could get into the graveyard?'

'Yes,' I squeaked 'They're all in there, the whole wedding party. And I'm sure they'll have tied the knot by now. So you've lost, see!'

The duke's face darkened. 'The game isn't over yet.'

And then he dragged me towards the gates, yelling at the ghouls to follow him.

In the moonlight I could see the clock on St Julian's tower. It was striking midnight. I gritted my teeth. We had an hour to get the rings back to Lena. But first I had to escape the duke . . .

'Hurry up!' he growled, dragging me faster along the path.

I glanced at the headstones, tall and white in the light. Some had people sitting on them, their ghostly occupants, I presumed. But they melted away as soon as they saw the duke. Angrily, he dragged me down the path and then along another until we reached a giant tomb, more the size of a shed than a grave. Across the top was engraved Bonti Family Mausoleum.

'Lena's family,' he growled. 'So where is she?'

As if in answer, a sudden streak of white hurled itself at him, crashing into his head. The duke let go of my arm and swatted the white light away. 'Irritating fly!' he spat, and the light crashed into one of the nearby headstones. Then I realised it was Charlie. The ghouls immediately surrounded him, clicking their cameras.

'No!' I gasped. But luckily Charlie was right. Cameras didn't work in graveyards.

But the duke wasn't done with us yet. He pushed the ghouls aside and snatched up Charlie by the throat. 'Where is she, boy? Where is your sister?'

'Somewhere you won't find her!' Charlie growled. And the duke immediately tightened his grip around Charlie's throat.

'Stop it!' I screamed, and I ran at the duke, head down, fancy shoes ready to kick him. But he flicked me aside easily. As I landed hard against a headstone, I skinned my knee. The sharp pain made me more angry than ever.

The duke smiled smugly. 'Do you want to die too, little girl?' he boomed. 'So you can be a ghost like your boyfriend!'

What? My face turned scarlet with embarrassment. I'm not sure what was worse. Being called a little girl, or the duke thinking Charlie was my boyfriend. Yuck! As if! I hurled myself at him again. And this time I managed to kick him with the pointiest part of my shoe. The duke shoved me aside. As I landed, I skinned the other knee. At least now I had a matching pair.

'Enough!' growled the duke. 'You lot can eat the girl,' he told the ghouls. 'But don't be litterbugs, put her bones in the bin.' Then he cackled with laughter and turned away, still clutching Charlie.

'Let go of me!' I yelled as a ghoul grabbed my arm. But my cries were drowned out by a sudden baying noise from the sky above. The ghoul instantly dropped me like a hot rock. And as I looked up I saw an enormous figure striding through the sky towards us, with three large hounds at its heels. The dogs were the size of bulls, with great jaws and massive teeth. As for the figure, I couldn't tell whether it was a man or a woman because its cloak hid its face. But the duke recognised the person straight away. He flung Charlie aside and walked over to greet the stranger. The ghouls meanwhile shrank back into the shadows, obviously frightened by the hounds, which stood at the figure's feet, glaring menacingly around.

I crept over to Charlie.

'Who is it?'

'A sky walker,' he whispered, his voice still tight from the duke's throttling. 'One of his spies.'

And then the duke let out a cackle of laughter.

'So the bird has flown. But not far!' he shouted. 'She's at St Peter's!'

'No!' gasped Charlie.

And the duke pointed at me. 'Careless words, cost lives.'

Charlie's eyes bored into me. And I bit my lip. The old woman in the baker's!

The duke meanwhile was rounding up his ghouls. 'St Peter's . . . now!' he yelled. 'And call the others too.' Then the air was filled with a deep whispering noise, as though a million people were all talking in low voices. I clamped my hands over my ears and Charlie covered them with his too. Then suddenly it stopped and the sky was full of black shadows, so many they momentarily blocked out the moon. In a breath they were gone and Charlie and I were alone with the dead.

CHAPTER 10

'It's all my fault,' I said, holding my head in my hands. I'd ruined everything.

Charlie shrugged. 'One of his spies was bound to find out.'

But I knew he was disappointed. Then a thought popped into my brain . . .

'Maybe Freddie's at the graveyard already. And if he is, then he and Lena will be safe inside, away from the duke and his cameras.' I glanced at the clock – 12.10. 'Maybe they could even get married *before* the thirteenth hour. Surely it wouldn't matter that much. If only we could warn them.' I glanced at the sky. 'Could we try and reach St Peter's before the duke?'

Charlie shook his head. 'They're adults, Jess, they can travel faster than us.'

I groaned. And just when I thought things couldn't get any worse, they did! There was a sudden shout. I looked up to see a young ghost standing in front of us. It could only be one person, Lena's fiancé, Freddie.

'Charlie,' he grinned. 'Thank goodness you're all right. Lena's been so worried. I've come to find you and make sure everything's okay.'

Charlie sighed.

Introductions were not necessary. Freddie was like the mirror image of Lena except he was a bloke, obviously. But he had the same storybook good looks – pale hair and kind face and eyes that sparkled like the beetle hearts on my dress.

'I knew exactly where to look for you,' Freddie went on. 'Up here, sneaking around under the duke's nose to get your sister's rings!' He smiled at Charlie and shook his head. 'Though really you shouldn't have flown off like that,' he said seriously. 'If the duke had got you . . .' He stopped as he saw our faces. 'Where is the duke anyway?'

And then it all came tumbling out. How the duke had found us, and discovered the truth about where the wedding was really taking place . . .

Freddie's shoulders sagged. 'Then it's too late.'

'Couldn't you just sneak in now?' I said desperately.

Freddie shook his head. 'St Peter's is like a box. There are no gaps. That's why we chose it. Once you're inside, you're safe. But getting in when it's surrounded by cameras will be impossible.'

I groaned, and then collapsed on a headstone.

'It's me who forgot the rings,' muttered Charlie, obviously trying to make me feel better.

I tried to think of something to say. As I did, I ran my hand idly over the writing on the stone. And then I felt a tingle under my fingertips. One of the words was familiar.

'Pocket,' I said softly, and then louder . . . 'Pocket!'

'What?' Charlie glanced down at the grave. 'Arthur Pocket – yeah, so what?'

'The human cannon ball!' I yelled, leaping to my feet. I glanced at my watch. It was a quarter past midnight now. 'There's still time!'

'What for?' Freddie floated over to take a look.

'Charlie,' I gasped, leaping over and grabbing his hands. 'Is Arthur Pocket a ghost? Like you, I mean.'

'Yes, he is,' said a lady's voice nearby.

I jumped. She was sitting on a tomb a few headstones away, and next to her was a tiger.

'Don't be afraid, dear,' she said. 'Old Buster is a real pussycat!'

'Except when he bites off your head,' muttered Charlie. And then in a louder, much more polite voice he called out, 'Evening, Tammy!'

'The lady climbed off her tomb and floated over. She looked about my gran's age, but she was wearing a black leotard, fancy tights and a really shiny top hat on her head. The tiger, all big paws and pointy teeth, padded after her.

Are you looking for Arthur?' she asked.

'Yes, I am,' I stuttered, keeping my eye on her big cat. 'Do you know where he is?'

'Down at the museum, I shouldn't wonder. He's never been one to hang around his headstone. He likes to be near his cannon.'

And then I remembered. 'It's in the museum, isn't it?' I knew I'd seen it before. We'd been to the museum on a school trip. Gordon Twigg had even showed us around. The cannon was right by the door when you went inside.

Tammy nodded. 'Yes, that's right, dear. Old Arthur can't bear to be apart from his cannon. Just like me and Buster, eh, old boy.' And she ran her hand over the tiger's head affectionately.

My eyes sparkled with excitement. 'Charlie!' I shouted. 'Don't you see – Arthur can help us!'

'How?'

'He's the human cannon ball, isn't he?'

Charlie nodded.

'The fastest one in the world?'

Charlie shrugged. 'He said he was . . .'

'We're going to find him and borrow his cannon. Take it out of the museum and get Arthur to show Freddie how to be a cannonball. Then we'll fire him over the top of St Peter's walls, straight past the cameras and into his own wedding.'

Freddie grinned at me. 'Cracking idea!'

Tammy shook her head. 'I don't like to be the party pooper, but the duke might still get you. He's very speedy with his camera.'

'But his ghouls aren't,' I said. 'The cannon will shoot Freddie out so fast; he's bound to miss him. And perhaps me and Charlie could create a diversion.' I glanced at Charlie hopefully. 'We'll run ahead of the cannon and try and get the duke's attention, and his ghouls too, giving Arthur time to fire Freddie over the wall.'

'I'm in,' said Charlie with a devilish grin.

'Me too!' shouted Freddie.

Even Buster gave a roar.

'Puss wants to play,' said Tammy with a shrug. 'So I guess we're in too.'

'I don't suppose anyone else in here would like to help?' I asked hopefully.

A dozen arms shot out of the surrounding tombs.

Charlie grinned at me. 'Looks like the Duke of Spooks has finally met his match!'

CHAPTER 11

I glanced at the clock. It was 12.25. Just over half an hour left. If the plan was going to work we needed to go now.

But as we prepared to fly, Tammy held up her hand . . .

'Wait! How will we get the cannon out of the museum?' she demanded. 'I mean, we ghosts can pass through walls . . . but a cannon?'

'I know a man who has the keys.' I said. 'He lives near here. And I'm sure I can get them off him.' I turned to Charlie. 'Have you got the wedding rings?'

He held out a skinny white hand. Two old gold rings lay in his palm.

'Maybe I should look after them,' I said, taking them from him. 'Just in case . . .'

He nodded, and then finally we were off.

As before, me and Charlie flew together. But this time we had an escort. I looked over my shoulder and tried to see how many ghosts were following us, but I soon lost count. They looked like your average bunch of dead people – mostly old grannies and grandads, I reckoned, with a few show folk mixed in. Charlie told me about them as we flew. There was Moustachio the strongman, who'd died from a septic toe. Eric the fire-eater, who was burned to a crisp after a bad attack of indigestion. Snuffles the clown, who'd drowned in his bucket. And Tammy, whose tiger had bitten off her head, though she didn't bear a grudge because the tiger choked and became a ghost at the same time as her.

As we arrived at Gordon's house, the ghosts lined up quietly on his lawn like large white gnomes, while Freddie and Charlie slipped inside to unlock the back door for me.

'Sounds like he's asleep upstairs,' Charlie whispered.

'Boy, does he snore,' I giggled, padding past him into Gordon's hall.

'That's not him,' said Charlie. 'It's his mum!'

I grinned. I'd met Mrs Twigg a few times and she was a tough old bird. It didn't surprise me in the slightest that she snored like a bloke.

'Where are you going?' Charlie added, as I headed for the stairs.

'The keys could be anywhere and we haven't time to look. I'm going to wake up Gordon and ask him to give them to me.'

'What!' Freddie gasped. 'He'll call the police.'

'I don't care. They'll never believe him. And besides, he owes me a favour. He's just jilted my auntie Glow. It was supposed to be her wedding day tomorrow.'

Freddie's face hardened. 'The scoundrel!'

Charlie shrugged. He obviously felt the same away about weddings as Andy did.

'Come on,' I said, tiptoeing up the stairs. 'Hopefully old Mrs Twigg's not a light sleeper.'

She was in the first room. Gordon was next door, lying on his back and sleeping peacefully. But not for long. The minute I saw him I felt a surge of crossness on Auntie Glow's behalf.

'Oi!' I said, poking him in the chest. 'Wake up, bog-head!'

'What? W-w-w-what's going on?' I suppose I was the last person he expected to find in his bedroom in the middle of the night.

'Don't shout! Don't scream!' I growled, in my best gangster voice. 'Don't do anything at all. Just sit there, shut up and listen to me.'

Gordon glanced anxiously behind me, catching sight of Charlie and Freddie hovering near the end of his bed.

'I want the keys to the museum. Where are they?'

'What?'

'You heard me. This isn't anything to do with you or Auntie Glow, or the wedding that you've ruined.' I glared at him. 'But I need those keys to help a good friend of mine. And if you don't give them to me, my companions here are going to haunt you for the rest of your life!'

As I spoke, Freddie and Charlie made their spookiest faces.

'Do the eye thing,' I hissed. And Charlie's eyeballs instantly shot out.

Gordon gasped and clutched his chest. For one terrible moment I thought he might be about to have a heart attack. Then I'd never find the keys.

'Look,' I said more gently now. 'Charlie and Freddie won't hurt you. They are ghosts, but friendly ones. Freddie's due to get married in . . .' I glanced at the watch. 'Twenty seven minutes, only a bad man has surrounded the graveyard where his fiancée is waiting. He can't get in unless we fire him over the walls using the old cannon that's in your museum. Understand?'

Of course he didn't! How could he? It was bonkers! I mean, can you imagine being woken up in the middle of the night and hearing such a ridiculous story. Nope. Me neither. But strangely Gordon didn't seem the least bit surprised. He reached for his dressing gown.

'Have I time to get dressed?'

'No!'

'Okay,' he shrugged. Then he climbed out of bed, and walked past the ghosts, over to the door. And for a second I thought he was about to leg it. But he didn't. He just reached up to the jacket that was hanging there, and pulled out a bunch of keys.

'Come on then,' he said. 'I suppose I'll have to let you into the museum myself. If I don't, you'll trigger all the alarms!' He puffed out his cheeks as though I was just an irritating nuisance, like a wasp or a fly or an ant . . . 'And anyway,' he grumbled, 'that cannon weighs a tonne. You'll need some help to shift it.'

'What?' It was my turn to be shocked. 'Are you saying that not only do you believe me, but you'll help me too?'

Gordon frowned. 'I'm a historian, Jess! Nothing about the past shocks me. And anyway, I've known

Arthur Pocket since I was a little boy. It was him who got me interested in history.'

'You mean, you've seen ghosts before?'

He raised his eyebrows. 'Why do you think you're special? The museum is full of them. Though I haven't been this close to one before.' He put on his glasses and peered at Charlie.

Charlie's face reddened slightly, and immediately he put his eyes back into their sockets. Then Gordon held up a hand. 'There's only one thing I won't do, and that's fly. I'll go and fetch my bike.'

And we were off again, with me, Charlie and Freddie hovering above Gordon (still in his dressing gown), who was cycling for all he was worth, while the others floated shyly behind us.

As we travelled, I told Gordon what had happened. About Lena coming to find me, and how the duke wanted to stop her from marrying Freddie, and how he ruled the town's ghosts with an iron fist, keeping them locked up in the show, zapping them whenever he felt like it. Gordon didn't say much, he just cycled on in silence. But when I told him how sad Auntie Glow had been when he dumped her, and why I had made my poster, he looked embarrassed . . . sad even. But there was no time to talk about his wedding. The watch was ticking. We had barely twenty minutes left.

CHAPTER 12

Many moons ago, the Sunny Bay museum used to be housed in a big building in the middle of town. There was plenty of space and the museum was free for anyone to wander round whenever they wanted.

'But all that changed when the building got bought by a local property tycoon,' explained Gordon, as he carefully unlocked the museum door. 'Roger Pilkington-Smith was his name and he decided to turn our building into flats, expensive flats for rich business people like him.'

'What!' I gasped. 'But that's him – the Duke of Spooks. The man who wants to stop the wedding.'

'Really?' Gordon frowned. 'He's a bad one, all right. Because of him, the museum had to move here – a building that's too small and too expensive. He owns it, you see. And he charges us a lot of rent to stay here.' Gordon punched in a code to switch off the burglar alarm. 'As a result we've had to start charging people to come in, and sell off a lot of exhibits to pay him. But luckily not this old girl,' he added, patting the cannon, which took up most of the museum's front lobby.

We all stood and stared. So this was the human cannon's cannon. It was enormous! The size of a Range Rover. It stood on a large metal platform, with huge rusting wheels at the bottom.

'Arthur Pocket built it himself, to look like an 1870s Turkish Howitzer,' explained Gordon. 'It's heavy iron, you know.'

Charlie nodded. 'I remember Arthur had a little steam train which he used to drag it into the ring. You should have seen it!'

Gordon tapped the barrel of the cannon. 'But we don't have the train. How on earth are we going to move it?'

'There must be a way!' I squeaked. 'It's not far. Just down the sea front a bit, so we're slightly closer to St Peter's. Then we can fire Freddie into the graveyard!'

It wasn't far. Not really. If you were strolling on a sunny day it would probably take less than a minute, if you didn't stop for an ice cream. But in the middle of the night, in the freezing cold, pushing an ancient two-tonne iron cannon with baying hell hounds and ghouls after you, it might take a bit longer. Except we didn't have longer.

'Where is Arthur, anyway?' Charlie asked.

Gordon shrugged. 'Inside the museum? He's quite friendly with a Viking longboat builder who moved in recently.'

'I'll go and fetch him.' Charlie darted off into the darkness.

Gordon meanwhile was unlatching the museum's double doors while the other ghosts zipped around, looking at the cannon and admiring the other exhibits.

'That's my granny's tea set!' I heard one say.

'Why have they got an old gas mask on show?' called another.

'There's Aunt Bessie's dining chairs,' shrieked a third.

'They don't get out much,' explained Tammy, whose tiger had nodded off at her feet.

I glanced at my watch. Fifteen minutes left. Where

was Charlie? What if Arthur wasn't there? He was the only one who knew how the cannon worked. Even if we managed to move it, without him to operate the thing we were sunk. I noticed Freddie was looking out into the night, his fists clenched, desperate to be with Lena.

'Come on!' I yelled, into the museum. 'Get a move on!'

Instantly Charlie reappeared, closely followed by a small, wizened old man. I had a good look at him. He had wild hair and a determined-looking chin. Not to mention slightly mad eyes. I looked nothing like him!

He stuck out his hand. 'Pleased to meet you, young Pocket,' he said to me. 'Charlie's filled me in on all the troubles. Too bad. Poor show. Terrible man, the duke.' He shook his head. 'Love your idea, though how you'll get Old Gertie down to St Peter's, heaven knows!'

'Old Gertie?'

'My cannon,' he said, whizzing past me to give it a quick spit and polish. 'A beauty, isn't she? Built her myself.'

But there was no time to admire his handywork.

Gordon had taken off his jacket and was rolling up his sleeves . . .

'Come on,' he sighed. 'Let's give it a go.'

And we did. All of us. Me, Gordon and the ghosts. The ones from St Julian's, and dozens of new ones who had popped out of the museum. The blonde-haired Viking boatbuilder. Some ancient-looking farm workers. A milkmaid. Several soldiers. And two rather posh-looking ladies with frilly frocks and powdery hair. But even with their help it was a disaster. Like trying to move a building. Even the great Moustachio, the strongman, didn't have any affect.

But as more ghostly apparitions appeared and joined in, there was a sudden jolt, and Gertie finally did begin to move.

'It's working!' I yelled. And it was. Sort of. Inch by inch, we began to move forward. But after five minutes of hard pushing we still hadn't even reached the front door.

'This is hopeless,' I groaned, collapsing on the carpet. 'We'll never get there in time!'

'How long do we have left?' asked Freddie anxiously.

'Ten minutes, maybe less.'

'Perhaps I should take my chances with the cameras,' he said, moving towards the door.

'No!' I yelled. 'Come on! We can do it!' And everyone took up the strain again.

But just then I heard some voices outside. For a second I wondered if the zombie ghouls had found us, but instead three human heads appeared at the door.

'Hey? What's happening?' mumbled one. 'Are you robbing the museum?'

The ghosts immediately shrank back into the shadows, out of sight.

Gordon sighed. 'Friday night party people,' he said through gritted teeth.

'What?' I said.

'Drunks,' he snapped. 'People out having a nice time, drinking too much beer.'

And then an idea came to me. 'Why don't we get them to help? If they're drunk, they won't remember it tomorrow.'

'No, Jess, they'll just cause trouble . . .'

But I slipped past him over to the door and poked my head outside. There were loads of them! A big gang of blokes with beer cans all gathered round to see what was going on.

'Hello,' I said cheerfully. 'We're trying to move this cannon to the other end of the sea front. It's a wager, you see.'

'What?' said one, a puzzled, muddled sort of expression on his face.

'A bet,' I said. 'I'm an orphan. And I bet all the other orphans' pocket money that we could move this cannon up the sea front before morning. A local businessman said we'd never do it. But if we can, we'll win a load of his money for the children's home. Will you help us?'

It was so silly not even a zombie ghoul would have fallen for it. But the ten big beery blokes swallowed it like a sweetie.

'Er . . . okay?' said one, rolling his sleeves up. 'Come on,' he called to his mates. 'Give the little girl a hand.'

I smiled, even though he'd called me a little girl, and stood aside to let them into the museum. Not one of them bothered to ask why we were really pinching a cannon in the middle of the night. They just dropped their beer cans, rolled up their sleeves and got stuck in. Gradually the ghosts reappeared, trying their best to look as human as possible. But the men didn't take any notice of them. After all, it *was* Halloween. I suppose they just thought they were people in fancy dress. Plus the men were all too busy bragging to each other about who had the biggest muscles, and who was the one really moving the cannon. And they were . . . really moving it – the rusty wheels began to trundle out of the museum door and on to the sea front.

'How long do we have left?' asked Freddie.

'Six minutes,' I mumbled.

And still we shoved. And as we did, others along the sea front joined in. Young women in disco clothes. Spotty students with their giggly mates.

'Must be a sponsored push for charity,' I heard one mutter.

'Where do we stick the money?' asked another.

'Down the barrel?' asked a third.

I didn't have the breath to say, 'No, don't stick coins in the cannon.' We all just kept shoving. And then more ghosts joined in. I recognised many of them from the show on the pier – the ghastly screaming bride, the mad axeman, with his axe tucked into his pants so he could push with both hands, even the gruesome bodies that had writhed on the wall spat on their hands and took up a place on the cannon to help push. And still more people joined us.

'Looks like a Halloween fancy-dress event,' I heard someone say.

'Yeah, I'll give them a fiver,' his mate said, shoving coins down the cannon.

And we carried on heaving. But suddenly there was no time left. And we were still too far from St Peter's. The final seconds of the midnight hour were passing through our fingers like sand.

'How long?' gasped Freddie.

I didn't have the heart to tell him. But just when I thought it was all over – another wedding ruined, another chance of being a bridesmaid, bulldozed – a strange thing happened. A rather ordinary-looking woman in a neat suit appeared next to me. She was about my mum's age, with short blonde hair and a warm smile, and in her hand was a notebook and pencil.

'On your way to Lena's wedding?' she asked cheerfully.

And then I noticed the sparkly purple aura around her shoulders, which scattered fizzy embers on the ground that hissed as they fell. And I knew she was a witch. I looked around but no one else seemed to see her. I swallowed hard. Could I trust her? Was she another of the duke's spies out to trick me? I looked into her eyes, but even if I had trusted her, I was far too puffed out to speak. Luckily I didn't need to. She tapped her nose, winked at me and then pointed at Lena's watch. I glanced down. The hand had stopped moving. Time had literally stopped.

'But how?' I gasped, looking up. But the lady had gone. I looked at the watch again. Still the hand didn't move. Had she really stopped the clock to give us more time?

'How long?' asked Freddie.

'Er . . . a couple of minutes,' I said vaguely. And then I felt a surge of excitement rippling through my bones. We could do it, we really could. 'Come on!' I yelled. 'We're almost there now. There's still time!' Though *how much* time there really was, I had no way of knowing.

CHAPTER 13

Just when I thought I'd collapse with tiredness, Arthur suddenly gave a shout: 'This will do! Stop here!'

And everyone gave up the strain and sank to the ground, exhausted. We were still some distance from St Peter's, about half a football pitch maybe. But Arthur said the cannon would work from here.

I peered into the darkness. Up ahead, I could see a cluster of dark shapes standing around the walls of the graveyard. It was the duke and his cronies.

Meanwhile most of the ghosts had slunk back into the shadows, leaving us alone with the human helpers.

'Er . . . thanks very much!' I said to them. 'We made it!'

'Is that it?' said a girl in a sparkly disco top. I think she was expecting a big finishing line, with party poppers and a press photographer or two. I just hoped she didn't meet the zombie ghouls.

I nodded. 'Yep! Thanks ever so much for your help. Me and my uncle Gordon are off home now, aren't we?' I said to Gordon.

He nodded. 'Oh yes, thanks for your help.'

Everyone looked a bit let down then, as though they didn't want to leave. But they soon drifted off . . . even the bunch of beery blokes staggered away, still arguing about who had the biggest muscles.

'Oh heck,' muttered Gordon. 'Look!'

He was peering back towards the museum. A police car had pulled up outside.

'I'm not sure how I'm going to explain this one,' he said nervously. 'But I'd better go and try . . .' And he strode off, back down the sea front, his dressing gown flapping in the breeze.

But I wasn't listening. I was watching the shapes up ahead. Now our human shield was leaving, I wondered how long it would be before the duke and his mates appeared.

The ghosts meanwhile had come back to the cannon. Arthur was talking softly to Freddie, explaining what he needed to know about being a human cannon ball. 'At least it won't matter if you muck it up,' smiled Arthur. 'Because you're dead already!'

It was a cheery thought!

Freddie climbed into the mouth the cannon, leaving his head peeping out of the top.

'Matches?' I suddenly said. 'Has anyone got matches to light the cannon?' I hadn't thought to bring any.

Arthur smiled. 'A human cannon ball doesn't really get shot out with gunpowder!'

I frowned. 'Then how?'

He tapped the metal barrel. 'There a giant spring inside. The gun powder's just for show.'

All the ghosts grinned. And Charlie giggled. I scowled. I hate it when people laugh at me. Surely I wasn't the only one who thought that. Just then I heard a shout.

'They're coming!' cried Tammy. And Buster roared.

Ahead of us, I could hear the baying of the hounds – the hell hounds! Cameras were flashing too. And the dark shapes were running towards us.

'Come on!' yelled Charlie, taking off into the air. Tammy and Buster and the others followed, filling the sky like flickering fireworks, darting hither and thither.

'Watch out for the cameras,' I called. But just then I felt a tingle on my wrist. I glanced down. Lena's watch had started ticking again and the clock on St Peter's chapel began chiming the hour. The thirteenth hour.

'It's time,' I shouted to Arthur. 'Now!'

He raced round to the back of the cannon and hauled up a lever. There was a strange metal winding sound . . .

'Are you ready, Freddie?'

'Yes!'

'Good luck, then,' said Arthur. And he heaved the lever downwards. As he did so, Freddie took off out of the cannon like a rocket – hurtling through the air, heading straight for St Peter's!

As he did, I heard a shout. I'm sure it was the duke himself. And the ghouls suddenly stopped chasing Charlie and the ghosts, and turned their cameras on Freddie instead. But it was too late. He'd already disappeared over the walls.

DONG! DONG! DONG!

The chapel bell was chiming the hour – the

thirteenth hour. We'd done it, and just in time! I clapped my hands with delight. And then I gasped. On my fingers were the wedding rings.

'We forgot to give Freddie the rings,' I groaned.

'I'll take them,' said Arthur disappearing round the back of the cannon to pull up the lever again. 'It's been a while since I've flown with Gertie, but you never lose the knack.'

'No,' I said. 'I'll go.' And as I spoke I saw a huge shape running towards us. It was the duke himself, his face like thunder. I began to climb into the cannon. There was no way Lena was getting married without her wedding rings, or me. This might be my one and only chance of being a bridesmaid, and I wasn't about to miss it.

'Quick!' I said. 'Help me!'

'What? Oh no! It's not safe. There's no net. You'll crash. You'll die!'

'I won't crash. Tony and Albert will catch me,' I said confidently. 'That's what they do – catch people. They've never dropped anyone before. They told me that.'

Arthur shook his head, horrified. 'No, I won't do it. It would be murder.'

'But I'm a Pocket,' I yelled. 'A Pocket Rocket. It's in the blood!' I crossed my fingers and climbed into the cannon. I just hoped I was right. That I really was related to Arthur. 'Please, do it now!' I pleaded. 'Otherwise, I'll be dead anyway – look!'

Sure enough, the duke was heading straight for us, roaring with anger. 'I'll snap your neck, little girl,' he screamed. 'Break it with my own bare hands!'

'Quick,' I squeaked again. 'Pull the lever!' I shut my eyes and shivered. It was cold inside the cannon.

'Wait,' called Arthur. 'You'll need this!' And he reappeared in front of me with a bright-red helmet. He strapped it under my chin and then raced back to the other end. 'Good luck!' he called.

And then BOOM! I was off. Except I wasn't. As the spring released, the barrel of the cannon jerked downwards and a horrible, mangled, clunking sound came from within.

'One of the coins must have jammed it!' shouted Arthur.

Then suddenly I took off, but instead of rocketing gracefully up into the sky like Freddie had done, I shot out forwards at half the speed I should have, just a few feet off the ground. And then disaster – I slammed right into the duke himself!

CHAPTER 14

Splat!

Thank goodness I had the helmet on. It was like hitting a brick wall. I bounced back off him, wildly out of control, hurtling back towards the cannon. Any minute I expected to be skewered on its barrel. But just in the nick of time, I felt a pair of ice-cold arms catch me, and I missed the cannon by millimetres.

'What were you doing?' Charlie cried, as we hurtled into the sky.

'I forgot to give Freddie the rings.'

We slowed down and landed. Charlie was puffed out, but he still had the energy to shout at me. 'You're mad! Do you want to get yourself killed?'

'No,' I snapped, feeling small, sulky and a bit silly.

'Don't you know why Arthur Pocket's a ghost?'

he yelled. 'It's because Gertie splattered him head first into a brick wall. And it wasn't a pretty sight!'

'I didn't want to miss the wedding.'

Charlie rolled his eyes and we glared at each other for a few moments.

'Forget it,' I said. 'I've got to get these rings to your sister. Come on!'

We raced down the sea front towards the cemetery. But as we passed the cannon we spotted something a few feet in front of it . . . a body, lying on the pavement. And leaning over it was Arthur.

I glanced at the body's face. 'The duke!' I gasped.

Arthur looked up nervously. Was it my imagination or was there excitement in his eyes. 'He's dead!' he said simply. 'Properly, this time.'

'Must have hit his head,' said Charlie peering down at him.

Gingerly, Arthur bent his head to the duke's chest and listened. He shook his head. 'Definitely no heart beat.'

'Shall I call an ambulance?' I asked.

'No!' they both said.

'But I killed him.'

'Not strictly speaking,' said Arthur. 'You just bumped into him. It was an accident.'

I was appalled. I'd killed a man. He might not have been a real man, or a very nice one, but he was still dead because of me.

'Will they lock me up?' I said in a small voice.

Charlie rolled his eyes. 'No! Everyone will be glad he's gone.'

'Definitely!' said Tammy, who had appeared next to us. And then a small crowd began to gather, mostly ghosts with a few lost-looking ghouls mixed in. Now that their leader was dead they didn't seem to know what to do.

But Tammy and the others did. They swiped the cameras from the ghouls' necks and turned them on their enemy. With a few dozen clicks, the duke's cronies had disappeared, leaving nothing but a slight smell of dead dog behind.

I glanced down and gasped. The duke's eyes flickered open, and the front part of him peeled away from his corpse and floated up to face us. He was a ghost – a super-angry one!

'You,' he thundered, reaching out to throttle me.

But before he could, I heard a sudden click! And all the ghosts froze. Even the duke.

'Let go of her,' said Tammy. 'Or I'll zap you!'

She was pointing a camera directly at the duke himself. He looked at her in shock and surprise. You see, up until then I don't think he'd realised what he'd become – a fully formed, fragile phantom!

The duke glanced down at his transparent body, and behind at his lumpen corpse, still lying conked out on the pavement and then he screamed:

We all covered our ears. It wasn't a pleasant sound. But then the crowd of ghosts parted and the ghastly bride from the haunted house ride stepped forward.

She was beaming delightedly, clapping her hands with joy. 'Oh, don't fret so,' she said, running to hug him. 'You're one of us now. I'll take care of you . . .'

Charlie smothered a laugh. 'Sad Susan,' he whispered. 'She got killed on her wedding day and her groom married her sister instead. She's been looking for a replacement husband ever since. She's always had a thing about the duke, though for some reason he's terrified of her!'

Sure enough, the duke began shaking and shuddering and swatting Susan's hands away. 'Not you. Not again!' he squealed. 'Go away. Go away, all of you!' And then he took off, floating up into the night with Susan following him, making kissy noises and whispering sweet nothings.

At that moment I heard another sound. The sound of singing . . . beautiful singing.

'All things bright and beautiful, all creatures great and small . . .'

'The wedding,' I gasped. 'We're missing the wedding. I've got to run. I'm the bridesmaid!'

At once I took off in my battered-looking bridesmaid shoes that were covered in ghoul gunk, with my bloodied knees and wild hair. Heck! I didn't even have a bouquet to carry. But I didn't care. I wasn't going to miss this wedding for anything. And then I felt cold hands clamp around my sides, and Charlie was lifting me up and over St Peter's wall, just as the singing stopped and the ancient old vicar stepped forward . . .

CHAPTER 15

'Who gives this woman in marriage?' said the wizened old voice, as me and Charlie slotted in behind Lena and Freddie.

Lena turned to me, and smiled a thousand thank yous. And Tony and Albert gave me a thumbs up. They'd caught Freddie. Of course they had. I knew they would.

'We're giving Lena away,' said Tony and Albert together. They took their sister's hand, kissed her on the cheek and then passed her hand to the vicar.

'Do you, Lena Louisa Bonti, take Freddie Farraday Fox to be your husband, to love and care for him as long as you both shall be?'

'I do!'

'And do you, Freddie Farraday Fox, take Lena

Louisa Bonti to be your wife, to love and care for her as long as you both shall be?'

'I do!'

Freddie slid a ring on Lena's finger. She put one on his. Then the vicar paused, and glanced up at the clock on the wall above. And he waited for a moment or two.

'What's wrong?' I whispered to Charlie.

'Wait and see!'

I looked at the clock and saw the time. It was the thirteenth hour. And it was now exactly thirteen minutes past the thirteenth hour on the thirteenth Halloween. And suddenly the graveyard was bathed in beautiful light. So bright I had to close my eyes.

'What's happening?' I squeaked.

Charlie squeezed my hand. Except it couldn't have been him, because the fingers were warm.

And then I heard the vicar's voice. 'I now pronounce you man and wife.'

I opened my eyes and gasped. Lena and Freddie were no longer ghostly apparitions; they were as alive as you and me. Their skin was pink and glowing. Their blonde hair shone golden in the light and their eyes sparkled with life and love. It looked like something from the final moments of a movie, you know the bit, right at the end when the soppy music begins and everything's come right.

'What's happening?' I asked, turning to Charlie. But he had changed too. His hair was now as black as a crow's wing and his blue eyes twinkled with mischief. Then suddenly he did something weird – he kissed my cheek!

'Oi!' I yelped, dodging away. I wasn't sure what was most shocking – him kissing me, or the fact that his breath was so warm.

But he wasn't the only one changing. All around me the wedding guests were transforming back into the humans they'd once been. Albert and Tony were poking and pinching one another. Charlie ran over to join in. Even the old vicar was looking at his hands and arms delightedly, seeing again his wrinkly old human skin.

'Amazing, isn't it?'

I turned, and there was the witch who had helped me by stopping the clocks. But she wasn't alone now. She was with Pallidia Black, the stitch witch. And I was glad to see Pallidia's chameleon was back on her shoulder, alive again!

I looked around. 'So this is why Lena had to be married at the right time?' I said.

Pallidia nodded. 'It happens every thirteenth Halloween. For thirteen minutes at thirteen minutes past thirteen, the dead walk among the living. Lena and Freddie wanted to marry as they used to be.'

I glanced at them. 'Won't they stay that way then?'

'No,' said the other witch. 'They'll soon change back. But the dead always live for the moment. Unlike the living, they don't worry about tomorrow, they just enjoy today.'

And they were certainly enjoying themselves now. The zombie band were no longer zombies. They were human musicians playing real instruments and all the guests were getting up and dancing – the show ghosts, the graveyard oldies and loads of others I'd never seen before. Even the shy fisher folk, whose graves we were jigging around, were popping up and joining in too.

'I'd like to interview you later,' said the blonde witch, pulling out a notepad again. 'It sounds as though you've had quite a night!'

I frowned. 'Interview me?'

She held out her hand. 'My name is Agatha Gum, editor of the *Darkington Times*. Pleased to meet you, Jessie Pocket. You'll be famous when I've finished with you!'

I wasn't sure what the *Darkington Times* was, but there was no time to talk because just then Lena seized my hand and hugged me close.

'You did it, Jess. You saved my wedding!' Then Freddie hugged me too and the three of us danced in a little circle to the crazy tunes the band was pumping out. And others began to join in too. Charlie took my hand, and then Tony and Albert appeared, and Arthur Pocket and Tammy, though thankfully Buster kept his distance.

And when the thirteen minutes was up, and all the spooks slowly began turning back into their ghostly selves, no one cared. They were all having too much of a good time. At some point Gordon Twigg arrived – to this day, I still don't know how he explained the cannon on the sea front to the police officers. And he's never told me. And although Gordon's not much one for parties, I'm sure I saw him doing a bit of 'dad' dancing in the corner.

Much, much later, Agatha came and interviewed me for the *Darkington Times*, which she said was a newspaper for unusual people like her and the spooks. She also introduced me to a shy man called Mr Kirk, who was wearing overalls and carrying a toolbox. She said he was going to be doing some work in Sunny Bay, correcting all the CCTV cameras.

'It's our wedding present to Lena and Freddie,' Agatha explained proudly. 'Pallidia and I have asked Mr Kirk to fit ectoplasm filters to all the cameras in town, so they can't zap the ghosts any more.'

'Not that they'll need them now the duke's a ghost himself. He'll do anything he can to have the things pulled down altogether.'

'But what'll happen to the show on the pier?'

'Without any ghosts, I can't see it lasting long, can you?' Agatha grinned. 'And I don't think Roger Pilkington-Smith would want it to now he's one of them!'

I don't remember going home. I just remember feeling tired, and climbing up on to one of the tombstones for a rest. And then shutting my eyes and dreaming of snow and a cool breeze whistling round my ears. But then suddenly someone was shouting loudly in my face . . .

'Wake up, dough-ball! Mum says if you're not downstairs in two minutes she's going to go ballistic. The wedding cars are waiting!'

CHAPTER 16

'What?'

For a second I wondered if it had all been a dream. But of course it hadn't. This isn't that kind of a story. It all happened, every word.

Andy gave me another shake. 'Mum's been calling you for hours.'

'What?' I looked around, astonished to find myself back home in bed.

'The wedding's back on!'

'What?'

Andy pulled at his neck tie uncomfortably. 'Look! See? I'm wearing a suit! The wedding's going ahead after all.'

I still couldn't make my brain work. 'But why?'

Andy was getting impatient now. 'Because crazy old

Gordon Twigg says he's made a terrible mistake and wants to get married after all!'

I hauled myself up on to my pillows and Andy gawped at me, a nasty smile spreading over his face. 'Look at your dress! Mum's going to go nuts!'

I glanced down and gasped. I'd fallen asleep in my bridesmaid's frock. Of course it wasn't my bridesmaid's frock any more. Not the one that had been made for Auntie Glow's wedding. It was the one Pallidia had created. Though actually it was just a crumpled purple mess now. I grimaced. How on earth was I going to explain it to Mum or Auntie Glow?

I threw back my duvet and staggered out of bed. My whole body ached and my legs very nearly gave way. I felt beaten up, either from pushing that crazy cannon, or more likely from torpedoing into the Duke of Spooks, killing him in the process!

'Why are you wearing your shoes in bed?' said Andy making a face.

I glanced down.

'And look at the green paint on them!'

I didn't want to tell him that it was ghoul gunk. I took a tissue from a box on my desk and gave my shoes a half-hearted rub. But the green wasn't budging.

Andy shook his head. 'You're going to be grounded for ever!'

But I didn't care. I was too tired. I went into the bathroom and looked in the mirror. I looked a fright. Like I'd been partying all night at the best ever Halloween bash. Which was kind of true. I glanced at the dark purple shadows under my exhausted eyes and the deathly pale colour of my face. I grimaced. I looked like a ghost! I picked up a comb and tried to get it through my hair, but there were so many knots I didn't stand a chance.

'Come on, Jess,' yelled Mum, rattling the bathroom door. 'We've got to leave now!'

And I headed out to face the music.

Mum didn't stop yelling at me until we reached the gates of St Julian's. Andy, of course, loved every minute.

'How could you?' Mum bawled. 'How could you ruin your beautiful dress like that!'

I didn't bother telling her how special it was, hand

made by a stitch witch using needle-spider cobwebs and sparkly beetle hearts.

'Auntie Glow's going to be so disappointed,' snivelled Mum, as the driver opened the car door for me.

But of course she wasn't. Auntie Glow couldn't have cared less if I'd turned up at her wedding wearing a six-foot funky monkey outfit. Because she was too busy having the time of her life. Somehow between her and Gordon they'd managed to get everything rebooked again. The church. The flowers. Even the horse-drawn carriage, which Auntie Glow and my grandad arrived in together, a few minutes after we got to church.

Auntie Glow looked amazing. Not because of the big white frock she was wearing, but because, just like Lena, she glowed with happiness. And Gordon did too; in a much quieter way of course.

Auntie Glow didn't notice my dress. She just beamed at me. And when I held her bouquet so she could take Gordon's hand, she gave me a little squeeze of joy. It was lovely to see and more than made up for some of the funny looks I was getting from the other guests in the church.

After the service we had to stand outside for the

photos. The sun was back and there wasn't a hint of the hailstones that had started the adventure the day before.

As I waited for my turn in front of the camera, I couldn't help but look around the graveyard and wonder where all my friends were. Lena and Freddie had told me they were going on honeymoon to somewhere called Screaming Sands. And Charlie and his brothers were probably back haunting the Grand pier, now the duke wasn't there to stop them.

'Sorry, I just need to change batteries,' called the wedding photographer. 'Won't be a moment.'

While he was rummaging in his bag, I tiptoed away, back down the path, the one that led to Lena's family tomb. And there it stood, the size of a shed, with their names clearly visible now in the daylight. I ran my hand along the front, and as I did I heard a chuckle from inside. Charlie! I knew it was him.

'Hello, dead head,' I said. And then I laid my bridesmaid's bouquet down in front of the tomb, so they'd know I hadn't forgotten them. 'Bye for now,' I whispered, and then I headed back to the church, passing Arthur's grave on the way.

Gordon met me halfway up the path. 'Your auntie Glow's just powdering her nose,' he said.

I smiled at him. 'Thanks for today,' I said. 'It means a lot to Auntie Glow.' I scuffed the grass with my green-slimed shoes. 'And thanks for last night too.'

'It's me who should be thanking you, Jess. Seeing what Lena and Freddie went through to be together made me realise how much I love your auntie Glow.' His cheeks reddened. 'And of course as a historian it was fascinating to meet such interesting people.'

I grinned.

'Have you ever thought of getting a Saturday

job?' he asked as we walked towards the church. 'The museum always needs helpers, you know.'

I quite liked the sound of that. And then Auntie Glow appeared and suddenly I was swept up in the day. And for the second time in twenty-four hours I had to work my bridesmaid socks off. There were people to meet and greet, and gifts to give out. And loads of younger kids that I had to look after. Then there was the disco and I had to help Auntie Glow change into another outfit for the dancing. And at last it was time for her and Gordon to go on honeymoon, and we had to wave them off. As she climbed into their car, Auntie Glow turned and waved her bridal bouquet. 'Catch it, if you can,' she called.

I smiled, but didn't try. After all, the girl who catches the bride's bouquet is supposed to be the next one to marry. And I definitely wasn't planning to get hitched any time soon (even though I quite liked the frock, the flowers and the horse-drawn carriage!).

It was much, much later and I was finally back home in my room, sitting at my desk where it had all begun.

I glanced down at the pile of paper and pens that I'd been using to make my Bridesmaid for Hire posters. As I moved them into a neat pile, one of the pages stuck out. It was a different colour to the rest and rougher round the edges. I pulled it out and discovered it was a newspaper, a rather ancient, crumbly looking one with a black border and old-fashioned loopy writing. It looked like it belonged in Gordon's museum. I unfolded it and felt a flutter in my belly. The title was the *Darkington Times*. And there, on the front page, was a black and white pencil drawing of a girl in a beautiful bridesmaid's dress. Me! Above, the headline read:

HELL'S BELLS!
BRIDESMAID FOR HIRE SAVES THE DAY!

It was my story. Every word of it, just as it had happened, just as I'd told it to Agatha Gum at the party last night. I grinned. How she'd got it into her newspaper so fast I had no idea! But it didn't surprise me. I folded it up and slipped it back under the pile of paper. Then I went to brush my teeth and get ready for bed.

As I climbed under the duvet and turned off the light, I actually hoped I'd hear Charlie's cheeky giggle in the darkness of the room, ready for another adventure. Then I stretched out my aching body in my deliciously cosy bed and decided sleep was a much nicer option. But as I closed my eyes a terrible thought suddenly burst into my brain. What had become of the other posters I'd made? What if other crazy brides had got hold of them . . . a werewolf bride, maybe. Or a vampire one, perhaps. Or what if Sad Susan had actually managed to convince the Duke of Spooks to get hitched!

I listened. What was that? I was sure I'd just heard a strange noise outside my bedroom window. What if they were out there now, lining up to grab me to be their bridesmaid? No way! I had to stop them . . .

I flicked on my lamp, leaped out of bed and reached for paper and pens.

BRIDESMAID NO LONGER FOR HIRE! I wrote in huge letters. Then I grabbed the sellotape, and stuck the sign to the window of my bedroom.

With a sigh of relief, I climbed back into bed, pulled the duvet over my head and shut my eyes tight. No matter who – or what – came calling, this bridesmaid was now definitely off duty, for the time being, anyway . . .

The scariest news there is!

Darkington Times

Today's wea
Drizzling
and teet
shattering

VOL. LXII NO. 35   SCREAMING SANDS - SPOOKY SUMMER SPECIAL   FREE

Exclusive: Spooky Sam Hay reveals all about her new book set in our ghostly town.

Q: Welcome to back to Screaming Sands, Sam. Pull up a scare — sorry, I mean a chair — in the Whistling Kettle café. Would you like a drink?

A: Oh . . . err . . . Snot Chocolate please! Or maybe something stronger. A Gin & Toxic or a Bloody Mary. Must keep out the cold! Oh, wait... I see they do milksnakes! Clawberry please!

Q: Super! I'll have champain. So what is it you like so much about this seaside ghost town?

A: Oh it's great. It's got everything the undead could ever want . . . rain, cold, dark — lots of dark! Did I mention the rain? Oh and then there's spiders . . . Enormous spiders!!! Hey...? Where are you going? ...Don't leave...STOP!

[Sam rugby tackles interviewer and sellotapes her to her chair]

Q: Sorry, Sam. I've only just moved here and I'm very easily spooked. What would you like to eat? I think I'll have ghoulash with a side of dready salted crisps.

A: Well, as this café is famous for i-scream, I'll have one scoop of shock-late and a scoop of vankiller please! BONE APPETITE!

Q: And to you! So, where did you get the idea for this story?

A: Er... um... well, [author searches the filing cabinets of her brain] ... I love the seaside, but I don't like sun or crowds much. So I tend to go on wet, cold days when no one else is around and it's easy to imagine a different type of customer (the pulse-less variety) hanging out there. Plus when I was a kid I always wanted to be a bridesmaid. But I didn't know many brides so I considered hiring myself out! I used to daydream about attending weird weddings!

Q: If you could be any character from your books, who would you be?

A: I love Jess. She impetuous and fiery! She does stuff without worrying about the consequences. Whereas I tend to leave the house with a giant bag bulging with stuff I might need, just in case. Stuff like spare clothes, snacks, money, passport, lucky pebbles, six blunt pencils, emergency mint cake, because you never know... Also Jess gets to fly and wear a dress made of cobwebs. Did I mention the spiders? I'd also quite like to be Brimstone, the chameleon from ATTACK OF THE BALLISTIC BLANKET. He's a shape-shifting magical lizard. Then I could be anything I want to be... dog, cat, giant woolly mammoth! Imagine!!!

Q: I'd I love to be Brimstone! Then I could shape-shift out of this sellotape. I've just heard that the dastardly Duke of Spooks has derailed all the trains out of Screaming Sands! Looks like we'll be stranded here FOREVER.

A: Oh, I don't mind staying. I love cold, wet, dark places. And spiders! And i-scream! Actually, my tummy's rumbling. Can I have another sundae? I've heard the 'Doris' is very good. Want to try one? Did you know it is named after a dead donkey?

Q: I did! I read all about Doris in THE DAY THE DONKEY DROPPED DEAD. She's my all-time favourite zombie donkey.

So what do you have in you giant bag to accompany you on your endless stay on this spooky beach?

A: I brought along a giant encyclopaedia, because I'm super nosey and always need to find out lots of things about a lot of stuff. I also brought Martin, our Cat. He's not at all useful. He's dim and scared of everything. But he is a black cat. So he'll help me fit in with the witchy folk staying in Screaming Sands. It's always a good idea to blend in with the crowd when you go on holiday - especially when the crowd could turn you into a two headed toad if they didn't like the look of you.

Q: What would you be doing if you weren't a writer?

A: I'd quite like to be magic. Is that a job? No. Okay... Librarian, then. But only if I can work in a small, dark, dusty old library that no-one ever visits, then I could just read all day, unbothered by people! Alternatively I love pencils, so could I be a pencil tester in a pencil factory please?

Q: Um... Oh! I've just heard they've put on a replacement bus service. You can go home! Don't worry about the bill – the folks at the Whistling Kettle Café say it's on the house as thanks for the screamingly funny books you are writing about the town.

More screechingly funny stories set in Screaming Sands (and find out how it all began for the seaside ghost town!)

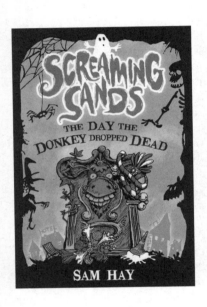

To find out more about Sam Hay and

discover other exciting books, visit:

www.catnippublishing.co.uk